FAST ENTRY

Guild eased the hammer back on his gun.

He put his hand on the doorknob and turned. It gave.

He knew he had to move quickly.

He opened the door, flung it inward, dropped to the floor in anticipation of the gunfire he hoped would go over his head.

Nothing.

He lay on the floor, left hand steadying right wrist, ready to get off a series of shots, when she said, "God, mister, you're not going to shoot me, are you?"

He got up and went inside.

GUILD

Edward Gorman

BALLANTINE BOOKS • NEW YORK

This book is in memory of my father,
who would have understood Guild.

They tried him for it back in '86, in a red brick courthouse just outside of Yankton.

The prosecutor, a plump man with the voice of an orator and the gaze of a hangman, told the press, "I believe this is one of the most despicable crimes ever perpetrated in the entire Dakota Territory."

The man on trial went by the name of Guild. He was six-two, blue of eye, gray of hair, with a knife scar on his cleft chin and a slight stiffness in his right knee from a boyhood riding accident. He might have been forty, he might have been sixty. You could not quite tell.

He had no money, at least not the sort good attorneys required, so the Territory was disposed to obtain one for him. Hampton was a man of twenty-three whose shingle had been out less than a year. He had the freckles and pug nose of an altar boy and the dull earnest voice of a high-school debater. Guild took one look at him and said, "Kid, I sure hope you don't get me hung."

The trial went three weeks. There was not a single extra courtroom seat to be had. They had to bring in spectators in shifts, so everybody got a turn. Women wept and men

1

cursed. Lynching was a subject much whispered about. The prosecuting attorney hooked his hands in his vest and strutted back and forth in front of the jury with the confidence of a pit bull closing fast on a kitten.

For his part Hampton did a lot of mumbling and standing abruptly up and then sitting right back abruptly down. The prosecuting attorney gave a performance worthy of a Shakespearean. Hampton sat there and riffled through law books as if studying up fast for a test.

The newspaper reporters, who seemed to know about such things, predicted a quick deliberation and in the end they were right.

The jury was out only two hours, just about the amount of time the journalists had promised.

The only thing the foreman did wrong was read the verdict as "Not Guilty."

A terrible hush ensued.

Then the mother of the little girl who'd died began sobbing. Harshly. Her grief was intolerable, not only for her, but for those who heard it. She was quickly removed.

The judge, a white-haired man jowly with age and indulgence, raised faded brown eyes over the bench and gazed down at Guild. "You're a free man, Mr. Guild."

Guild just sat there and stared at his hands.

"Free in body," the judge said. "But I pray to God you're never free in your mind, Mr. Guild. I pray to God that you're doomed to face what you did for the rest of your life."

With no little disgust, the judge raised his gavel and banged the trial to a close.

Chapter One

Danton was a town in the northwest part of the Territory. It was getting to be impressive. There were poles for electricity and poles for telephone service. There was an opera house and a library and a Montgomery Ward's of two full stories if you counted the wagon repair shop on the ground floor. There were stagecoaches and carriages and buggies filling the streets, and there were even two shining steel tracks plied by a horse-drawn trolley with a pealing little bell to get bicycles and pedestrians out of its way. There was no doubt about it. For the Territory, which had seen the last of the Indian wars only a few years earlier, this was becoming a mighty fancy place.

Guild rode into Danton on a late May day with dusk streaked gray across a sinking red sun and a rising silver quarter-moon. He sat on a muddy dun, leading a prisoner astride a roan. The man, chunky in a plaid drummer's suit, was handcuffed to the saddlehorn.

As it was a Saturday night, Danton was noisy with the sound of pianos and alcohol and girls you could rent for waltzes and polkas and a few other things as well.

"Could use a beer," the prisoner, a man named Maloney, said.

Guild kept leading them down the street that was still muddy from last night's rain.

"Hell, I'm gonna get ten for sure," Maloney said. "Goddamn prison farm. You wait and see. Swore I'd never work the soil once I left it after my Pappy died, and now look what I've goddamn gone and done." He paused. "How about it, Guild? That beer?"

Guild turned around and looked back at the fleshy man. He couldn't quite resist smiling. "You're some prisoner, you know that? All you've done since I picked you up two days ago is complain. I didn't know it was my job to see that you were comfortable."

Maloney smiled back. "You're kind of a gentleman, for a bounty hunter, I mean. Figured if I fussed long enough, I might just talk you into a beer."

Guild asked a local for directions to the sheriff's office. A block away was a store that sold both groceries and beer in buckets. When they reached it, he reined in his dun and then reined Maloney in, too.

Guild got down and stood stretching a moment. He wore a black Stetson, a tailored black suit coat, a boiled white shirt, gray serge trousers, and black Texas boots. A .44 was strapped around his waist.

He said to Maloney, "You know how tired I am, Maloney?"

"How tired?"

"So tired that I'm crazy enough to go in there and get us a bucket to share."

Maloney, who was fifty, grinned—his dirty face like a kid's.

"But I'm also so tired that if you tried to get away, I wouldn't chase you. I'd just go for that Winchester repeater in my scabbard over there and put a hole the size of a bottle right through your back."

"Hell, man, you think I'm gonna run off when there's a beer in the promise?"

Guild went in and got them a bucket, and when he came out he took the handcuffs off Maloney. Then they sat together on the steps of the place and smelled the new grass and the fertile mud and the apple blossoms of this spring. They listened to the wrens and robins and barn owls of this gathering night and watched the stars begin to shine.

"Pretty stupid goddamn thing you did," Guild said. "Robbing the hotel where you were the desk clerk."

"Well, my Ma always said that there was two things God never give the Irish."

"What's that?"

"Noses and brains."

They both had a good laugh on that one and then they finished the bucket, Maloney making a big thing of belching. Guild put him back up on the saddle and in the handcuffs and took him the rest of the way to the sheriff's office.

The deputy got Maloney put away then came back into the big front office with its glass case of rifles and shotguns and its two mahogany desks and its west wall full of a Territorial map and its east wall full of WANTED posters.

"How the hell he get beer on his breath?" the deputy asked. He wore a khaki uniform so clean and so creased it would have made West Pointers envious. A crisp campaign hat sat on top of his narrow head. He had a pinched, cross face and a fancy new leather holster for his Peacemaker.

"I gave it to him."

"You gave your prisoner beer?"

"Sure? Why not?"

"Why not? Are you crazy?"

"Not that I know of."

5

"Beer. Shit." The deputy shook his head and then went over and sat behind the desk. He had to fill out a form saying that Guild had duly delivered the WANTED man. Guild needed this in order to collect the reward of three hundred and fifty dollars.

"What's your name?" the deputy asked, not looking up from his writing.

"Guild."

"You got a first name?"

"Leo."

"Leo Guild," the deputy said to himself as he wrote it.

Guild waited for him to glance up. For a little explosion of shock or superiority to form in his eyes. But maybe, finally, people didn't remember anything about it any more.

The deputy placed a piece of carbon beneath his writing so that when he got finished, he gave Guild one copy and he took the other.

The deputy nodded to the wooden door beyond which lay eight cells. "He a troublemaker?"

"He look like it?"

"You got a mouth full of smart talk, don't you?"

Guild sighed. "I guess I didn't much care for your remark about my giving him beer."

"Well, you got to admit it's a pretty strange way for a bounty hunter to be treatin' a prisoner."

"Where he's going, he won't have beer for a long time."

The deputy grinned. "Nope. I guess about the only thing them boys up in Territorial prison got is each other."

Guild folded the form in half and put it in the pocket of his shirt and said, "Thanks, deputy. Appreciate it."

Then he went to look up a church.

Chapter Two

St. Mary's sat in a copse of pines on the southeast edge of town, just up from a beef kill that left the stench of blood on the air.

There were buggies and bicycles in the dirt parking lot. Saturday night was Confession night, when not only the town folks came but also the farmers and farmhands and sometimes the people from even further out, the trappers and residents from the dwindling Army posts.

The church was cut of stone and stained glass. Inside, the air was rich and sweet with incense. Guild, Ohio born, had been raised Lutheran. He had not yet quite become used to all the ritual: the crossing yourself, the holy water, the genuflecting. But a few years back the nightmares had become so bad, the little girl's face so vivid, that he decided to try Confession. Not Baptism, not Holy Communion, not Confirmation. Just Confession.

The votive candles glowed red and green and yellow and cast long shadows deep into the pews where stocky immigrant ladies sat with kerchiefs covering their heads, the men not allowed to wear anything on their pates in the House of God.

7

Guild took a pew in the back, sat, and waited his turn as people went up into the Confessional. The penitents whispered into the waiting stillness then came out again. Sometimes you could hear what the people said, and sometimes you could hear what the priest said, and sometimes both their voices got so low you knew what was being said must be terrible indeed.

Then Guild went in and knelt down. In the cubicle of darkness he could hear the priest cough, and then Guild said, "Bless me Father, for I have sinned."

"Yes, my son?"

Guild had found a catechism a year ago so he could at least get the form down. In Confession you had venial sins and mortal sins. You confessed the venial ones first, sort of working up to a climax with the mortal ones.

Guild hurried through the lesser offenses, taking the Lord's name in vain, lusting after married women, becoming angrier with people than he should.

The priest said, "Those are your sins then?"

"Yes, Father."

"You've made a good examination of conscience?"

"Yes, Father."

"Then I will give you your penance."

As he did.

Guild said, "There's one more thing, Father."

There was a pause, a sly pause, as if the priest had known all along that Guild was not saying what he'd come to say.

"There is another sin you want to talk about?"

"I don't know if it's a sin, Father. But it bothers me. It bothers me very much and sometimes it won't leave me alone at all."

Guild had had three bad nights of the dreams and one could hear them now in his weary voice.

"Tell me, son," the priest said. "Maybe I can help."

8

Guild told him.

At Harrington House, as the landlady primly informed him, you were expected to get your own hot water from the kitchen stove downstairs and carry it upstairs to the bathroom you shared with six other boarders. Towels, she said, you found in the hallway closet.

So at nine-thirty that Saturday night Guild sat naked in a tin tub of hot sudsy water, reading a newspaper story about all the trouble President Cleveland was having with tariffs. He had just finished the letter column, which was filled with missives decrying the notion of the Territorial Government to breaking up the Territory into sanctioned states. The fear seemed to be that there were enough laws on the books already and that if statehood became fact there would be thousands of more laws to contend with.

Confession had helped. It always did.

Guild, after scrubbing his face, his neck, his ears, his armpits, his testicles, and his feet, was ready for clean clothes and dinner in a place where you could gaze upon women whose images you kept with you forever, like goodluck charms.

He had just leaned back in the tub, putting the paper on the floor and a fat brown cigar in his mouth, when he began hearing the irritating sound of new leather shoes pacing back and forth outside the bathroom door.

Somebody wanted in here.

Guild cursed. He liked to lay back with his eyes closed and inhale deeply of the stogie and just sort of float for a time.

Now there was somebody out there with squeaky leather shoes. Somebody in a hurry to get in here and take his place.

Guild tried to relax for a few more minutes, but it was

impossible. He got up and dried off and put on the clean, boiled white shirt and the black suit jacket and the gray serge trousers and the new white socks and the shined black boots. In the mirror he examined his clean-shaven face and his combed gray hair and the gray mustache he'd grown last year.

The last bather had left two things on the sink: a bottle of fig laxative and a bottle of red water to splash on after shaving. Guild had no need of the former but he did indulge himself in the latter.

Then he went over and opened the door and got his first sight of the man in the squeaky shoes.

"You're goddamn lucky I didn't just come in here and pull your ass out of there," the man said.

What was comical about this was the man's size. He was maybe five-five, five-six at most, slight as a girl, handsome in a dark-haired, theatrical way that was accentuated by the gambler's outfit he wore: red silk vest and severely cut black coat and lace shirt and string tie. He looked to be only in his mid-twenties but the frenzy and grief in his dark eyes said that these had been hard years.

"You're drunk," Guild said.

"What?"

"I said you're drunk. Are you deaf, too?"

"What the hell's my being drunk got to do with anything?"

"If you weren't drunk you'd be able to see that I'm about twice your size and just about ready to put my fist in your face."

"It's Saturday night."

"I know it's Saturday night."

"It's Saturday night and I'm already late and you sit in here hogging the goddamn bathroom all to yourself."

Guild decided to let it pass. He hefted his warbag and pushed past the man.

10

But he couldn't resist a last comment. "You better sober up and cool that temper of yours, or you're going to run into somebody who isn't as even-keeled as I am."

All he got in return was "I don't remember asking you for any advice, padre."

Then the man took his towel and his shaving kit and went into the bathroom, kicking the door violently shut with his heel.

Guild frowned.

Then he dumped his warbag in his room and went to the restaurant the boardinghouse woman had told him about.

Chapter Three

It might have been New Year's Eve instead of a soft spring night. There was a twelve-piece orchestra playing music that caught you up in its festivity immediately, and there were waitresses whose lovely skin glowed in the light of the massive chandeliers and the Rochester lamps. Women in pink gowns and white gowns and blue gowns that cost as much as a working man's wages floated around the three floors of the restaurant on the arms of men who talked in loud, important voices about finance and politics and local matters as if their opinions alone could change the course of things. Most of the men wore black evening suits with white percale bosom shirts and white bow ties. The plump, pink-faced maitre d' put Guild on the second balcony, as if he wanted to get him as far out of sight as possible.

Guild had a good steak and boiled potatoes and three glasses of wine. Then he had a cigar and sat back and listened to the music from the band, which was just below him on the ground floor. This was society music, the sort played at cotillions. Though it made him tap his feet, he wanted to have his wine and his cigar and hear fiddles on the sweet night air. He could listen to fiddles for hours.

Finally, predictably, he got tired of looking at and listening to the walruslike men around him with their air of money and malice.

But he was not ready to go back to his room. In the past four months he had tracked four men, one after the other, almost without pause. He had money. He needed to relax. He was still feeling good from Confession.

When a waiter came by, Guild stopped him and said, "Is there a veranda?"

The waiter nodded and pointed. "Good view of the hills, too."

"Thank you."

Guild picked up his check, left coins for his waitress, and then pushed his way through all the chatting and chittering society people.

The veranda was on the other side of tall, curtained French doors. The fresh air was like a balm. Guild stood there with his cigar. He looked first at the quarter moon with its nimbus that promised rain and then at the eastern ring of piney hills lovely in silhouette. Then his gaze dropped to the streets below. Lamplight gave the business section the feel of a civilized eastern town, the buildings newly built and carefully tended, the boardwalks wide and clean.

He stayed outside fifteen minutes and was ready to go back through the mob of party-people when he heard the argument. He walked down to the opposite end of the veranda and looked down on the back of the restaurant. There were a line of garbage cans and a buckboard standing horseless. There was a garage with an open door. Inside you could see stacks of canned goods in cardboard boxes.

In the middle of the back area stood three people, two

men and a woman. One of the men had his fist cocked. He was ready to use it. Guild recognized the man as the one with the squeaky shoes back at the boardinghouse who'd wanted into the bathroom.

The other man was tall and dark-haired and in evening clothes. Even from here Guild saw a smirking arrogance on his face.

But it was not the men who held Guild's eye. It was the woman. Girl, really, he supposed. She couldn't be more than twenty. Guild did not know if he believed in angels, but she made a strong case for their existence. She had blond hair done up in a crown of braids the way Swedish girls wore them sometimes. Not even the alley light could disguise the simple, startling beauty of her face or the slender perfection of her body in a white pinafore.

The punch was about to be thrown when the girl stepped in between the two men.

"Earle, Earle, you got to calm yourself down," she said.

She was speaking to the boardinghouse man. From her pleading tone Guild could not guess her relationship to him. He could have been husband, lover or brother.

The man's fist faltered. "He owes us, Annie, and he knows it." If anything, he was even drunker than when he'd confronted Guild.

The other man said, swelling himself up, "I have to get back inside to my wife and friends." This was how gods spoke to mortals.

With that, he nodded to the girl and stalked off, back into the restaurant.

Earle took one swing at empty air, then another. "You should've let me hit him, Annie."

She laughed a sad laugh. "You always forget, Earle. You're real pretty, but you ain't very tough."

"What'd I tell you about ain't?" Earle snapped. Then,

"Not very tough?" Earle's voice was now a shout. "You're just afraid that once I get going, I won't be able to stop. That I'll kill somebody."

As if to prove his point, he slammed his fist into the side of the buckboard. Immediately he shouted in pain and sank to the ground.

Guild watched as Annie dropped down next to Earle, holding him, as he started fitfully to cry in the hesitant way men cry.

"He owes us the goddamn money, Annie," Earle said, drunk and crazy and forlorn sounding. "I'm sick of lettin' rich people like him push us around."

She didn't say anything, just held him and rocked him and occasionally kissed his face and then shushed him and rocked him some more.

Guild still could not fathom their relationship. She seemed to be mother, mate, and guardian all in one.

Finally, they got up, Earle wobbling, and somehow managed to move out of the light and down the alley and out of sight.

Guild finished his cigar and threw it over the veranda and then went back into the restaurant. All the same people were there spending more on drinks than you could make in a month at a sawmill or slaughterhouse. He left.

On his way back to the boardinghouse he found a saloon and had three nickel schooners of beer, enough to ensure that he'd sleep well.

In his room, he lay on his bed and thought of the comforting words the priest had uttered in Confession. Then he thought of the woman, Annie, he'd seen earlier tonight. The thought of her gave him an odd, almost pleasurable sense of loneliness.

*   *   *

He had no idea how long he'd been asleep when the noise came up from the street.

He woke and grabbed the .44 he'd put on the nightstand.

Down near the business district, four blocks away, there was the sound of shotgun fire.

He cursed. Sleep for him was fragile. Once awakened, he rarely slept again.

He found his pocketwatch and checked the time. It was not quite one o'clock. He might find a workingman's saloon open by the railroad tracks. The law was usually lax on such places closing down strictly at ordinance time.

He washed his face in the basin, combed his hair, put on his clothes, and went out into the spring night.

He was two blocks from the shopping area when he saw men come running from the alley across the street, carrying torches and rifles.

"You there!" one of them shouted. "Stop!"

Guild kept his arms loose and his hand clear of his gun so they would have no reason to fire.

There were four of them, townsmen rather than farmers or plainsmen, in good suit jackets and shirts. But they smelled of whiskey and sweat, and in the flickering light of the torches their eyes were wild and dangerous.

One of them, a puffy, balding man, lowered a Remington right at Guild's chest and said, "What's your name, stranger?"

"Guild."

"What're you doing out on the street?"

"I was going to have myself a beer."

"At one o'clock?"

"I'm just traveling through. The gunshots woke me up. Figured a beer would help me get back to sleep."

"You know a man named Earle Hammond?" a lean man in a striped dress shirt and suspenders asked.

Guild thought. So that was it. The man's temper has finally gotten him into trouble.

"No."

"You sure?"

"I'm sure."

"He doesn't look to know anything, Simon," a swarthy, potbellied man said. "We'd best start searching the alleys again." He glanced at Guild. "Sorry for the trouble, mister."

"No trouble."

"Come on," the swarthy man said.

The two men who'd questioned Guild looked reluctant to leave him. They obviously didn't believe, or didn't choose to believe, the explanation he'd given them for being out on the street this late.

The truth was, Guild wouldn't have believed it either.

There was a roundhouse down on the southern leg of the railroad tracks. And where there was a roundhouse there was inevitably a saloon that was the province of railroad men.

Guild got a schooner and then went over and sat at a table and watched two men finish off an intense game of eight ball.

"You sonofabitch," the redhead said whenever his opponent made a shot.

When the redhead made a shot, the grayhead didn't say "You sonofabitch." He said, "You bastard." They never missed saying it. It was like some kind of religious ritual.

Guild got tired of it and started looking around. A few men played pinochle, but most of the dozen or so stood at the long bar and ate hard-boiled eggs or pickles and told lies about their early days of laying track. Everybody here, it seemed, had had vicious battles with Indians. One espe-

17

cially drunken man told of fighting off a band of Atakapas up in the northern part of the Territory. If so, Guild thought, the Atakapas had come a long goddamn way. Usually you found them in Florida.

It was about Guild's third schooner when they took to telling tales of gunfighters, and Guild gave up on them entirely. Yellow paperback novels and lying journalists had created a breed of men who did not exist. Doc Holliday, for instance, had emptied a gun six feet from a man and failed to hit him once. Jesse James had failed to wound a bank teller at near point-blank range after three shots. They were pretty scary marksmen, all right, the gunfighters.

He went back to watching the game of eight ball.

"You sonofabitch," the redhead said as the grayhead clacked in the six ball.

Then the front door slammed open and there stood a fat, fastidious, white-haired man in a dark cashmere suit, a derby hat, a Prince Albert beard, and a sheriff's badge the size of a small plate. Even in forty-five degree weather, he wore black leather gloves. Guild knew who he was. Cornell Baines. At one time he had been one of the highest-salaried lawmen on the frontier. He had also been a Union soldier in Guild's platoon and it could be said that they had been friendly if not exactly friends. Guild had heard, over the past ten years, that Baines had become a highly paid and respected lawman in troubled towns he helped put to rest. Behind him came the deputy that Guild had earlier turned Maloney over to. The deputy had a Winchester. He looked eager to use it.

"I'll be damned," Baines said.

Guild smiled. "I never had much doubt about that."

"Karney here said there was a bounty hunter in town, but he didn't say who it was."

Guild put out a hand. They shook. Baines said, "A fellow named Robertson over at the bank was shot. We think Hammond did it while trying to rob the place. He must have gotten scared and run away after he saw that Robertson was dead.''

"The money safe?" the bartender wanted to know. "Most everybody's money in this town is in the vault."

"The money's safe. As I said, he just took off running, apparently. The vault wasn't even tampered with. Now we want to get this Hammond before he can get out of town."

"You just wait till we catch him," the deputy said. He was agitated, frenzied, like a hunting dog eager to tree its victim. "You just wait."

Guild said, "Real high caliber of lawman you've got there, Cornell."

Baines laughed. "Karney? He just gets a little overanxious."

"Apparently, a lot of people get that way in this town. I was stopped by some men on the way over here."

"Robertson was a well-liked man. Had a lot of friends."

"You sure this is the best way of going after Hammond, a bunch of drunk men running loose?"

Baines sighed, waved Karney away. "Go have yourself a drink, deputy."

Karney scowled at Guild, moved away.

Baines sat down at the table. He could have been the star of a Wild West Show. "Actually, all these men running around is Frank Cord's idea, not mine."

"Who's Frank Cord?"

"His father is the wealthiest man in Danton. Frank is the president of the bank, his father's bank."

"You always do what Frank Cord tells you?"

Baines smiled. "I've got things nice here." Something dark crossed his eyes. "Wife died a while back, consumption. Now I'm just a lawman looking for an easy time of it."

"And this is the place?"

"Long as you mostly do what young Frank wants you to."

"Mostly?"

"There's a judge here, name of Harnack. He has a saying, 'I'll do the right thing if you shame me into it.' "

Guild laughed and sipped his beer.

"You lend a hand?" Baines said.

"Afraid not."

"Why not?"

"Mobs scare me."

"Me, too, actually."

"Then call them off."

"Can't."

"Frank Cord?"

Baines nodded.

"Tell him you got shamed into it."

Baines said, "That doesn't always work."

"It's worth a try."

"This Robertson really was a well-respected man hereabouts. A lot of people want this Hammond fellow, with or without Frank Cord's urging."

"I wish you luck, then."

Baines said, "You ever see anybody from the platoon?"

"Nope. Sort of lost touch."

"I heard about what happened to you. The little girl and all."

Guild sighed. "I guess a lot of people heard about it."

"Could have happened to anybody."

"Seems to have happened to me, though."

"Sorry my deputy's such a shithook," Baines said. "He's a cousin of Cord's."

Guild grinned. "Why doesn't that come as a shock?"

Even standing up, Baines looked like a Bill Cody imitation about to take a bow. "Maybe we can have a drink or something tomorrow."

20

"I'll probably still be in town."

"Good."

Baines nodded his good night then went over to Karney. "You ready?"

Karney nodded to Guild. "He ain't goin', huh?"

"No," Baines said, "no, he isn't."

Karney, knowing Guild was listening, said, "Figures."

Guild did the only thing he could. Shook his head over what a sorrowful sonofabitch Karney was. Then he went back to finishing his beer.

Chapter Four

The landlady had baked earlier in the evening. On the way up the stairs to his room, Guild smelled cherry pie. He thought of how good a slice of pie and a glass of milk would taste.

From down the block he heard shouts. The mob was still out. Guild had seen how situations such as this one inevitably turned to lynching. As a young man up in Blackfeet country, he'd seen some farmboy troopers get heady on Army beer and then go lynch themselves an Indian they'd said had raped a settler's daughter. A trooper himself in those days, he'd tried to stop them. They'd knocked him unconscious. In the morning he rode out and found where they'd strung the young buck up. He cut him down and never forgot the almost comic glassiness of the corpse's eyes and the overwhelming stench of the carcass. He wanted no part of any mob.

At the top of the stairs he heard snoring and moaning. Most of the boarders were older people who made older-people noises. As the years passed, even sleep became a chore.

He was two doors down from his own room when he

heard a noise that did not belong in this hallway or this night.

Behind the door on his right, he heard the sound of a body bumping against a piece of furniture. A scraping sound.

Instantly, Guild crouched and pulled his .44 from its holster.

He had a strong idea of who had made the noise—Earle Hammond, who'd probably come back to get his belongings before fleeing. Without much luck at all he could easily lose himself in the forests and mountains and desert of the Territory. All he had to do was elude Sheriff Baines and his men for this night, and by sunup they'd never be able to find him again.

Guild put himself against the door. Listened.

From the other side of the wood he heard ragged breathing. Fearful breathing.

He eased the hammer back on his gun.

He put his hand on the doorknob and turned. It gave.

He knew he had to move quickly.

He opened the door, flung it inward, dropped to the floor in anticipation of gunfire that he hoped would go over his head.

Nothing.

He lay on the floor, left hand steadying right wrist, ready to get off a series of shots, when she said, "God, mister, you're not going to shoot me, are you?"

It wasn't hard to tell she was crying.

He was sweaty, shaking, angry.

He got up and went inside.

From the moonlight through the sheer white curtain suspended in the breeze, she was a silhouette tucked up into the head of the bed. The pinafore was gone. She wore a white shirt and a brown vest and butternut pants and riding boots. As his eyes grew accustomed to the shadows, he saw again how beautiful she was.

"You going to shoot?" she said again.

"Where is he?"

"Ain't here." Then she said, "Shit."

"What?"

"Earle told me not to say ain't, and it's just what I said."

He almost smiled. Her face was so classically beautiful, it misled you into thinking she was some kind of exotic romantic creature like those the serials in *Godey's* were always about. But she wasn't. She was a plains girl and a hard, untutored one at that.

He went over to the bed and said again, "Where is he?"

She moved as far away from him as she could get without falling off the bed. The room smelled of whiskey and smoke. It had a bed and a bureau and a basin. There was a small stoneware water dispenser and a hook rug on the floor. It was like dozens of rooms Guild had slept in. The girl made moist sounds. Her tears were running down.

"They're going to find him and they're going to lynch him," Guild said.

"Oh, no! Oh, God!"

"Tell me where he is, and I'll do everything I can to get him into jail and keep him safe."

"He didn't kill that man. I promise you, he didn't!"

"Where is he?"

"If I tell you, he'd never believe me that I was just trying to help him. He don't trust people. Not at all."

Guild put his .44 away. "If he doesn't trust me, I'm afraid he won't be alive by dawn. I've seen some of the men looking for him. They're in pretty mean spirits."

"He didn't kill that man," she said again.

Guild stood and looked at her. She had leaned a little more into the light now and he could see how tears had

24

puffed up her eyes. She was even younger than he'd guessed. Maybe seventeen, eighteen.

"He your brother?"

She shook her head.

"Your husband?"

She shook her head again.

"What is he, then?"

"My partner."

"Your partner in what?"

"Magic act."

"What?"

Given the circumstances, it was the most improbable thing she could have said.

"Magic act," she said. "We wouldn't have stayed here in Danton at all, except Johnston kicked us out of the circus. You ever heard of the Johnston Brothers Circus?"

Guild shrugged. "I guess."

"Well, there ain't really any brothers. There's just the one Johnston. Fenton Johnston. But he always said it sounded more impressive to say Johnston Brothers. Anyway, Johnston caught Earle playing cards again so he kicked us out."

"Cards?"

"Earle's real good with cards. He kept winning all the money the carnies had so Fenton would always get mad because the carnies would always get mad when they lost their money."

Fast as she talked, crazy as she sounded, it made sense. At least sort of.

Guild said again, "I'd like you to tell me where he is."

"Can you see what I'm holding up?"

"No."

"Then let me get in the light better."

She got in the light and he got his first prolonged look at her, and he could never recall seeing a girl more lovely.

25

She held out a heart-shaped locket that she wore on a thin gold chain around her neck.

"In here's a picture of my ma. At least the man who raised me said it was my ma. Anyway, whoever she really is, I believe in my heart she's my ma, so it's the same thing."

"Yes," Guild said seriously. "I guess it would be."

"There ain't nothing that's more holy to me than this locket. Can you understand that?"

Guild nodded.

"So right now, I'm going to do something I've never done before."

"What?"

"I'm going to give you my sacred word on this locket."

"All right."

She got up off the bed and stood next to Guild. She couldn't have been five feet nor weighed ninety pounds. "I'm holding this locket. You see?"

"I see."

"And I'm closing my eyes."

"All right."

"And right now, mister, I'm swearing to you on everything that's holy—I'm swearing to you on this locket of my ma's—that Earle, he didn't kill that man. I promise you he didn't. You believe me?"

What the hell else could he say? "Yes, I believe you."

"Good," she said. "Now we better go get Earle before that lynch mob gets him."

Chapter Five

Annie led Guild down a maze of alleys, left then right, right then left. Dogs yipped at them; wet laundry on clothes lines smelled clean in the night. In a house or two lamps burned.

They came to an industrial area of buildings that looked crude and temporary. Factories. A shoe factory, a wagonworks, an ironworks, a plowworks, and a creamery. You could smell engine oil and grease and sour milk. Guild said, "This is a long walk for an old man like me." He was out of breath.

"You really an old man?"

"Sometimes I feel like it."

She angled her head sideways, as if assessing him carefully. "Sometimes you look like an old man and sometimes you don't. Isn't that funny?"

"That's downright hilarious." He nodded to the dark and looming buildings. "You sure you know where you're going?"

"On the other side of those factories is an old barn. He's in there."

"Good. Let's go."

She put a cautionary hand on his arm. "I don't want you to go in with me. He'll just try to shoot you and then you'll shoot him. He ain't always a nice man, but he's taken care of me, mister. He's taken care of me real good."

"I'll wait outside the barn for you to bring him out. All right?"

She nodded. "Maybe I should have brought his carpetbag."

"Is that what you were doing back at his room?"

"Yes."

"Well, he won't be needing it, at least for a while."

She put out her hand. "Feel that."

He took her hand and held it.

"Isn't it awful?"

"It's awful," he said.

"You ever felt a hand shake like that?"

"No. I can't say I ever have."

"Are you making fun of me?"

"Nope."

"My hand really is shakin', isn't it, mister?"

"No doubt about it. Your hand is really shaking."

He still couldn't match her odd ways with her classically beautiful face. She was a damn strange girl. He said, "Let's go."

It took them ten minutes to reach the barn, which sat in the middle of a shallow growth of hardwood trees. The barn had apparently once housed some kind of small factory. Various rusted engine parts were strewn all over the ground out front. But the building had been left to the elements. The wood had begun to rot. It leaned so far to the left it looked about to collapse. There were the sounds of owls and coyotes in the night but nothing else.

Guild said, "You sure he's in there?"

"He wouldn't leave without me."

She said it with such absolute faith that Guild was touched. It had been more years than he remembered since he'd put such faith in another human being.

"I'm going in now."

"All right," Guild said.

"You keep your promise and wait right here till I bring him out." It was a command.

She touched her locket and set off.

He watched her run across the grass. It was wet with dew and shone silver in the moonlight. She was nothing more than a silhouette.

The barn door creaked when she opened it. Then she disappeared inside.

Guild took out his .44. No matter what kind of convincing she did, he expected trouble from Hammond. The kid was drunk and scared, and that made him very dangerous.

Guild was standing there watching the barn door when he heard something make a squishing sound on the damp grass.

He sensed in an instant what had happened but by the time he turned around, it was too late to do anything about it.

The long barrel of a Peacemaker caught him hard across the back of the skull, and he went down to his knees, fighting blackness.

Then a boot came up and caught him on the side of the head, just below the temple, and he could no longer fight the darkness.

All he could do was let it come and overwhelm him and take him wherever it led.

"God, mister, are you all right?"

Guild got one eye open. He smelled kerosene and rat shit and damp earth.

Annie held a lamp over his head and said, "Mister, can you hear me?"

He opened both eyes. "I can hear you."

"God, you didn't come around for a while."

"How'd I get in here?" By now he'd figured out he was in the barn. He'd also figured out who hit him.

"I drug you. 'Fraid I kind of got your clothes dirty."

"Where's Hammond?"

Guild heard the hammer on a pistol being eased back, and then another figure came into the circle of light Annie's lamp created.

Hammond, looking dirty and frightened, said, "Hammond is right here."

"Annie tell you about the mob?"

"I didn't kill him."

For the first time, Guild sat up. Slowly. He'd been hit harder many times before, but nonetheless his head hurt him now. He said, "If I had time or the inclination, kid, the first thing I'd do is stand up and push in your face the way I should have back in the bathroom tonight."

Hammond smiled. "Seems you're forgetting who has the gun."

"Kid, that gun doesn't mean squat. Not with that mob out there."

Annie said, "He didn't kill him." She touched the heart-shaped gold locket. "I made him put his hand on the locket and swear to me he didn't. Right, Earle?"

Hammond looked embarrassed by her reference to the locket. "She's got it right, Guild. I didn't kill him."

"Who was the man you argued with behind the Center Stage Restaurant tonight?"

"How the hell'd you know about that?"

"It doesn't matter. Answer my question."

"He's the president of the bank."

The local benefactor's son, Guild thought. He remembered how the sheriff, Baines, had described the man with such ironic contempt. "What were you arguing about?"

"He owes me four thousand dollars."

"Why?"

Hammond looked at his Peacemaker and said, "Seems I should be asking the questions, Guild, not you."

Guild was tired of being threatened. He helped himself to his feet. For a moment the pain came like a piece of lightning across the back of his head. He was irritated with trying to help a punk like Hammond. "Either use that goddamn thing on me or put it away," Guild said, nodding to the gun.

"He's right, Earle, put it away. He's our friend. He really is."

"Friend, my ass," Hammond said, but he reluctantly tucked the gun into his waist.

Guild thought about walking out. But he looked at Annie and how scared she was, and he knew he couldn't.

"I'm going to ask you some questions, Hammond, and if you want me to help keep you away from that mob, you damn well better answer them. Understand?"

"Oh, he understands, mister. He does. Really."

Hammond glowered. Obviously he did not like girls making his decisions for him.

"What were you arguing with Frank Cord about?"

"We had a poker game."

"And?"

"And he lost two thousand dollars to me. He looked me up night before last and asked if I wanted to play double or nothing, just the two of us, blackjack was what he had in mind, so I said yes. I'm damn good in blackjack."

"You won."

Hammond nodded.

"But he won't pay you?"

31

"He says I can't prove that he owes me the money and that if I try to collect he'll have me thrown out of town."

"Can you prove where you didn't kill the man at the bank tonight."

In the lamplight, Hammond shook his head. Miserably. "I—I was real drunk and I—I went over there to get my money. And he was there with Robertson . . . talking about something . . . and that's about all I remember."

Guild said to Annie, "Where were you?"

"Mister, by that time I'd given up on him. I was tired of arguing."

Back to Hammond. "So you went there alone?"

"Yes."

"And you don't remember anything?"

"I . . . guess not."

Guild said, "You need to be in jail."

"What?" Hammond's head snapped up.

"It's the only safe place for you and we'd better get you there fast. The longer the mob looks for you, the uglier it's going to get."

"No!" Hammond cried. He started to pull the Peacemaker from his waist, but Guild slapped him once across the mouth, hard enough to back him up three feet.

Guild pulled the gun from the man's waist and said to Annie, "Where's my forty-four?"

"Over there."

"Get it."

"You really think you should take him to jail, mister?" She sounded lost.

"I can't protect him otherwise."

Hammond had started to cry. "I didn't kill him, Guild, I really didn't."

Guild said, "You'll be safe in jail, Hammond. You've got to believe that. If the mob isolates you before we get you in a cell, they'll hang you for sure."

32

Annie started crying, too. They were like brother and sister—scared, scruffy drifters. The Territory was full of people like them.

Still snuffling tears, Annie got Guild his .44 and gave it to him, and then she went over and held Hammond much as she had behind the restaurant tonight. Mother, mate, friend.

She stroked his face and his head and his shoulder.

Finally, she said, "We better listen to him, Earle. We really better listen to him."

Chapter Six

A train pulled into the depot and people got on and off. The last of the taverns were closing up. In the livery a doctor was pulling a new colt into life. It was another night in Danton.

In the sheriff's office, Baines sat behind his desk and looked up at Guild.

"I appreciate this," Baines said.

"It wasn't something I planned."

"You may have saved this town a lot of grief."

Guild shrugged. "I'm not sure he killed that banker."

Baines tried a smile. "I wouldn't tell that to that crowd right now."

Guild put a boot up on the edge of a chair and leaned forward and said, "I want you to tell me something."

"What?"

"You wouldn't have any funny idea about letting the boys roam around tonight getting their hands on him?"

Baines sat there and sighed and said, "I'm not an old whore, Guild."

"Meaning?"

"Meaning, like most other smart people in Danton, I do

favors for the Cord family—but that doesn't mean I don't still have some pride."

"So you're giving me your word?"

"Jesus, Guild, you can be pretty goddamn insulting when you come right down to it."

Guild sighed. "Don't go getting dramatic on me, Baines. I just want you to tell me you're going to protect the kid."

"Well, of course I'm going to protect the kid. I'm a lawman, aren't I?"

"Then that's all that needs to be said." Guild nodded to the lockup behind the door.

Baines said, "He say anything to you?"

"He said he didn't do it."

Baines smiled. "Now there's an original tale."

Guild rolled a cigarette from a sack of Bull Durham. "Can he get a fair trial in this town?"

Baines shrugged. "He can always get a change of venue."

"He's got a girlfriend," Guild said. "She'll want to visit him in the morning."

"No problem with that."

Guild took off his Stetson and wiped his gray hair. "This is way past my bedtime."

"You go on home. I'll make sure everything is all right."

"I didn't mean to hurt your feelings."

"About what?" Baines said. But of course he knew damn well about what.

"About you not being a good lawman."

"In El Paso they paid me eight thousand dollars for three months work. I'd say my work kind of speaks for itself."

Guild stared at him a moment and said, "So I didn't hurt your feelings?"

Baines stared right back at him. Then he laughed with

his big white theater teeth and said, "Of course you did, you sonofabitch, but I'll be damned if I admit it."

"Just make sure the kid is all right."

"He'll be fine. Except for his hangover."

Guild nodded and said good night and left.

There was a café that stayed open all night, over by the roundhouse. That's where he'd promised to meet her.

She wasn't there.

Guild asked the Indian man sweeping the floor if a young white woman had been waiting in there. The Indian said yes, but that Ruby Gillespie had been there and taken her away.

"Who is Ruby Gillespie?"

The Indian, short and paunchy in denim shirt and pants, nodded out the door. "Editor of the *Chronicle* down the street."

Guild thanked him and went out the door. By his pocketwatch it was nearly three-thirty A.M. The sweet odor of horse dung mixed with the mud of the street. Guild was tired. But he had to see the girl and tell her that Hammond was all right.

The *Chronicle* was not much more than a doorway wide. It sat between a shoe shop and a pharmacy. Inside its smudgy window a kerosene lamp showed a messy single-room office. Two desks were cluttered with hurricanes of paper. A flatbed Washington Hand Press dominated the rear of the office. Type trays, ink rollers, and a single bale of white paper filled up the rest of the place.

Annie and a thickset woman in a brown tailored two-piece walking suit sat at one of the desks. The woman had short iron gray hair and dark eyes that even from here shone with real compassion. Annie sat in a straight-back chair and talked and cried. The woman wrote in a pad.

Guild tried the door and found it unlocked and pushed inside. A bell above the doorway announced his arrival. The place had the pleasant smell of ink and wood pulp. The *Chronicle* was obviously in the midst of getting out a new edition.

Annie, seeing him, jumped up from her chair and rushed over to him. "Is he all right?"

"He's fine."

The woman got up and came over. "I'm Ruby Gillespie, publisher of the *Chronicle*. At least I have been since last fall when my husband died of consumption." The pain was still in her voice.

Guild offered his hand and received a gentle one in return.

"We've got an edition coming out tomorrow afternoon," Ruby said. "I want to get her side of things before I go over and hear what Frank Cord is going to claim."

Her tone of skepticism interested Guild. "You don't think Cord will tell the truth?"

"Far as I know, Frank Cord's never told the truth in his life."

"How about his father?"

"Mason? Different story."

"He's honest?"

"He is what he is. Right or wrong, he built most of Danton. Only time I can't deal with him is when he has to cover something up his son has done."

"She thinks maybe Earle didn't kill him, mister," Annie said.

Guild frowned and made sure Ruby saw his frown. "You got a place she could sleep?"

Without hesitation Ruby said, "Sure. Upstairs."

"Then why don't you take her up and put her to bed. Then come back down here."

She caught his tone. She said, "I'm not much for taking

orders. My husband, Eugene, found that out over the years. I bore five children and won a medal for marksmanship at every county fair for five years running. Plus I'm the only newspaper editor in this part of the Territory with an actual high-school diploma."

She was getting angry, and Guild couldn't help but smile. He liked her pride even if he disliked the way she was filling Annie with false hopes.

"I apologize for the way I sounded," Guild said.

"Good," Ruby Gillespie said, "apology accepted. Now I'll get the girl to bed."

Before she went out the door, Annie turned around and said, "You promise me he's going to be all right, mister? You promise me?"

"I promise you."

"Then I'll be able to sleep."

"You need sleep, Annie," Guild said.

Ruby Gillespie returned five minutes later.

"You like bourbon?" she asked.

"Not unduly," Guild said, "but a shot or two right now would be nice."

"That's what I was thinking."

"It would also give you the chance to tell me about Mason Cord and his son."

She laughed. "Oh you're going to regret those words, Guild. I can jabber most of the night about Frank Cord."

So she got them some whiskey and two glasses, and she did just what she said she could do, jabbered most of the night.

She started out by saying, "Now I don't think it's feminine for a lady to swear, you understand, and every time I heard one of my daughters do it I got the soap out right away, so if I happen to call that sonofabitch Frank Cord a sonofabitch from time to time, I hope you'll forgive me."

Guild smiled. "I suppose I could find it in my heart."

She tilted her glass, let the whiskey work its way down her throat, and then started in.

"Frank Cord was a ladies' man, a bully, and a cheat. Growing up in Danton, he was in constant trouble and if not for his father's sending him East to military school, he might have been in serious trouble for setting fire to a shack in which an Indian had died.

"From his own father, Mason Cord had inherited some small holdings, which he in turn had built into a small empire here in the heart of the Territory, owned mostly by the McKenzie fortune. Unfortunately, Frank Cord, the next in line, proved mostly worthless. His father had set him up in several businesses, including a haberdashery, a furniture store, and finally a gun shop. He'd failed at each of them, preferring to spend his time entertaining young ladies and hanging around with gamblers.

"He's married to a woman of good enough virtue," Ruby explained, "but he spends a lot of his time up in the Timbers." The Timbers was a small resort where the wealthy and the reckless of the Territory gathered for cards and women, away from the proper eye of their respective communities.

"Why did his father put him in charge of the bank?"

"Because at the time, the bank was just a minor holding. But Mason has been gradually falling to Alexander McKenzie, and now the bank's about his only holding."

Guild shook his head. "Frank Cord sounds pretty much like dust, I agree, but why do you think he'd be lying about the Hammond shooting?"

She poured them some more bourbon and sighed. "I don't know, Guild, I mean I can't give you a reason."

"You just don't trust him?"

"I just don't trust him."

Guild helped himself to the bourbon. "I saw Hammond tonight. He could have done it."

"Shot a man? You sure?"

Guild nodded. "Annie would say different, I know, but he was drunk and mad. It isn't exactly a new story."

Ruby raised her eyes. "That poor kid." She shook her head. "But I can see why she'd like him. He took her out of a bawdy house."

"Where?"

"Kansas City, I guess. She said she started there when she was nine."

Guild made a face. He thought about her and her eyes and her grief.

"Said she went to the circus one day and saw Hammond doing a magic act and then she went right up to him and asked if she could go with him. She was twelve."

Guild finished his whiskey. "You giving me a little lecture?"

"Probably."

"Just because he helped Annie doesn't mean he didn't shoot the banker tonight."

"No, I suppose not. But then Frank Cord is involved in this, so I sure wouldn't want to bet on it."

He stood up and put his hand out and took her shoulder. "You serve good whiskey."

She smiled. "I noticed you seemed to kind of like it."

He tipped his hat. "See you in the morning."

"So long, Guild." she yawned. "I guess I'm getting tired, myself."

He found a café open and had potatoes fried in fresh grease and three eggs and five strips of bacon. Then he had two cups of coffee with some bourbon poured in it and a cigar. Then he got up and walked the rest of the way back to his boardinghouse just as a rooster started going and going good.

It took him less than five minutes to fall asleep once he shed his clothes and slipped underneath the quilt.

He had been asleep three hours when the banging started on his door.

Tired, it took him awhile to make certain that the knocking was not part of a dream. He rubbed his face and then bolted from bed. He grabbed his .44 and went to the door.

On his way there he noticed that a lovely spring day filled his window. He smelled hyacinths outside his window. A robin perched on his windowsill.

He got the door open and there stood Ruby Gillespie.

"You better come over, Guild. I can't get her calmed down any, no matter what I say."

"What happened?"

"Her friend." The climb up the stairs had winded her. She was trying to get her breath.

"Hammond?"

She nodded.

"What about him?"

"Got despondent, I guess."

"Despondent?"

"Isn't that some story?"

"What story?"

She caught her breath. "They're saying the Hammond kid got despondent over what he'd done and then hung himself."

Chapter Seven

On the way over to the *Chronicle,* Ruby explained what happened. Or at least what she'd been told had happened.

Guild just kept listening and not believing. The more she talked, the worse he felt. And he knew why.

He was sorry the kid, Hammond, was dead, but he was even sorrier for Annie—and sorrier for himself.

Because now he was going to have to face Annie.

The commercial district was noisy with people and wagons and trains as Ruby and Guild turned the corner to her office. The excitement was easy enough to see. People stood on corners and in doorways and over on the green of the town square and talked about everything that had happened in the past eight hours. There was a sense in the Territory that civilization was not only inevitable but good— yet most people still enjoyed the blood-quickening thrill that only violence brought.

There was a room above the newspaper office. They went up steep, dusty stairs and came to a landing. When they reached the top, Ruby said, "Maybe I should go in with you."

"No. It's my responsibility."

Ruby watched his face. "It wasn't your fault."

"Of course it was my fault."

"You just thought you were turning him over to the law."

Guild's jaw began to work. "Some law."

"You don't think he killed himself?"

"It's a possibility, but a damned convenient one."

And with that, Guild turned the knob easy, in case Annie was asleep, and went inside.

A red and blue patchwork quilt covered a small cot, above which sat a picture of Jesus with a yellow glow around his head. On a stand next to the cot stood a table lamp with a multicolored glass shade and a copy of *Century* magazine. Sunlight came through the southern window and shone on the bare wood floor. Dust motes tumbled in the light.

Annie was under the quilt, her face swollen from crying, clutching a small doll with a white porcelain face.

He started to back out of the room, but his boot squeaked on a board.

She woke instantly.

At first she was obviously confused—much as he'd been when Ruby had come to get him—glancing around at the strange room and then at Guild.

Then, terribly, he saw the look on her face that he had dreaded seeing.

She began sobbing—a breathless, horrible sound—and flung the doll at him.

"You promised me he'd be fine! You promised me, Guild!"

Then she leaped up from the bed, still in her butternut pants and white shirt, and came over to him and slapped him. "He was the only one who treated me good my whole life! The only one who never ran out on me!"

This time she kicked him as well as slapped him. Kicked

43

him a clean shot in the knee that made him bite his lip. But he didn't say anything. He deserved this and much worse.

"You just as good as killed him yourself!" she cried, and sank down to the floor at his feet. "You just as good as killed him yourself!"

All he could do was stand there and stare with dead eyes out the window at the blue day with its yellow sunflowers and sweet breezes that made no sense in light of what had happened.

Then she wrapped herself around his legs and clung to him because she had absolutely nobody else in the world to cling to, and he knew it.

She sobbed until he thought she would be sick, alternately wailing Earle's name and then cursing Guild for turning Earle over, and then she went into a kind of trance, her eyes lifeless as those of the doll that lay broken in the corner.

He lifted her up and carried her to the bed. He started to lay her back down so she could get some sleep, but she put her arms around his neck, holding him with sudden child-like need. So he just sat on the edge of the bed, holding her, feeling her tears on his own cheek, holding her with great and fragile care as if she was the most sacred thing he had ever held. Then he began to rock her softly, the way she'd rocked Earle, rocking her and beginning to hum an old tune his mother had hummed to him back in Ohio.

In a while she quit crying altogether, and then at last came the small sounds of her snoring.

Twenty minutes later, Guild walked up to the crowd that had gathered in front of the red brick sheriff's office.

Many of the people held pads and pencils, testament to how many papers flourished in each town of the Territory. Ruby had told him there were eleven alone right here in

Danton and that when they ran out of white wood pulp, which was shipped in from the East, they printed on brown wrapping paper and that readers were thankful for even that.

Guild reached the crowd. Karney stood in front of the door, flanked on either side by two more deputies. He had on a crisp new uniform. He had a shotgun in his right hand. So did the other two.

Karney said, "Now why the hell don't you people just go across the street to the saloon of your choice and we'll call you when the sheriff is ready to give a statement. All right?" He would have sounded official except for the whining sound that undercut nearly everything he said.

"How'd he hang himself?" one of the editors asked.

"How'd he hang himself? Abe, what the hell kind of question is that?"

"With a belt or rope?" Abe said.

"Oh, I see," Karney said. He shrugged. "With a belt, I guess."

Guild spoke up. "How does a man go about getting a belt in a cell?"

"Well, if it ain't the hero," Karney said. "Boys, this is the man who found Hammond for us."

"Leo Guild," one of the editors said. Obviously he knew who Guild was and what was in his past.

Guild said, "You didn't answer my question, deputy,"

"I ain't supposed to answer questions, Guild. That ain't my capacity. That's the sheriff's capacity."

"Then I want to see the sheriff."

"You can't see the sheriff."

"Why not?"

"Because he gave me this shotgun and he put me out here in front of the door and he said the only person I was to let in was somebody who worked in this here office."

Guild felt his mouth begin to go dry and a buzzing

45

begin in his ears. He was always like this just before he erupted. A kind of furious blindness overcame him.

The crowd sensed it, too.

Karney's shotgun hadn't been able to move them back but Guild's anger did.

"Then tell the sheriff to come out here."

Karney found that very funny. "You think I'd go in there and ask the sheriff to come out here? What kind of peckerhead do you think I am?"

Guild moved. He smashed in the deputy's nose with his fist, then he brought his knee up into the deputy's groin. Karney's face was bloody. He clutched his testicles as Guild slapped off his silly goddamn campaign hat and grabbed his hair and slammed the deputy's head against the doorframe. You could see the deputy's eyes dilate and then go white. The deputy was unconscious.

Guild let him slide to the floor, and then he went on inside.

He hadn't gone more than two steps across the threshold when the ham-actor figure of Sheriff Baines aimed a 10-gauge at his chest and said, "You try any of that jayhawker shit with me, Guild, and I'll kill you right on the spot. I mean it now. You just goddamn calm down."

Guild didn't doubt him at all.

"Now close the door behind you and get in here, and we'll sit down and do some talking," Baines said.

Guild said, "You gave me your word, Baines."

Baines snapped right back, "You think I let him hang himself?"

"He had a belt."

"Only through oversight."

"What the hell does that mean?"

"It means that dumb goddamn bastard Karney didn't take his belt off him."

"That's convenient."

46

Baines said softly, "I gave you my word, Guild."

"Yes, and you can see how much good it did."

Baines sighed. "I got called away to a meeting."

"Who called you away?"

"Frank Cord."

"Leaving his cousin Karney here."

Baines said, evenly enough, "Yes, leaving his cousin Karney here."

Guild said, "What the hell are you doing in a town like this, Baines?"

"Don't get pontifical on me, Guild. You of all people."

Baines's words were harsh enough to make Guild listen. Guild said, "For what it's worth, I guess I don't really think you had anything to do with it."

"You guess?"

"Right now I wouldn't swear to anything. Not for sure." He took out his Bull Durham. "You question Karney?"

"Of course."

"And?"

Baines shrugged. "I think you could probably pretty much guess what he said."

"He was sitting out here and didn't hear anything?"

"Boy seems to have some kind of hearing problem."

Then Guild remembered Maloney. "The prisoner I brought in. He must have seen something."

"Karney took his statement."

"Karney did? Why not you?"

Baines sighed. "Because he wouldn't talk to me."

"You're the sheriff."

"Goddammit, Guild, ease off."

They sat and smoked and glared at each other a full minute, and then Baines said, "Look, Guild, you know some kind of bullshit is going on here and so do I."

"Is that supposed to make me feel better?"

"No, but it should tell you that I'm not a part of it."

"Then you're going to help me find out what's going on?"

Baines said, "I've got arthritis fairly bad in my right hand."

"What the hell's that supposed to mean?"

"It just means I'm old and afraid of getting turned out in the winter like some animal."

"We're all afraid of that."

"I've got a nice thing here in Danton. You can't blame me for wanting to keep it."

"You're wrong, Baines. I do blame you now that Hammond's dead."

Baines sighed again. His wide, white-maned head bowed a moment. When he looked up, he said, "Why don't you go back and talk to Maloney? I'll stand guard here so Karney doesn't get in."

"You think Karney paid him off?"

"That and scared the hell out of him."

Guild looked at Baines and said, "You're a better man than this, Baines. A lot better man."

Guild opened the heavy door and went on back. Instantly there was a damp smell and the odors of urine and sleep and rotted food.

There were four cells, two on each side. On the wall of each was a high, barred window. You wouldn't have a hard time hanging yourself, if you really wanted to.

Maloney lay on a bunk, reading a magazine.

When he peeked around the edge of the pages, he broke into a smile.

"Hey, Guild, how are you?"

Guild nodded.

"Just thought I'd come back and see how you were doing."

Maloney made a rubbery face. "This is probably going to be paradise compared to Territorial prison."

48

"You'll be all right, Maloney." He paused, looked around. "Hear they had some excitement last night."

"The guy who hung himself?" Maloney crossed himself. "I don't go to Mass or nothing anymore, but I still think that's the fastest way to get yourself to hell. Suicide, I mean."

Guild took out the makings and rolled himself a cigarette. "You didn't try to stop him?"

"I was asleep."

"It didn't wake you up, huh?"

"Hell, when I get to sawin' logs, Guild, nothin' can wake me up."

Guild leaned against the bars and got his cigarette going, and then he said, "I wouldn't trust Karney." He paused then said, "Somebody promised you something, didn't they?"

"What?" Maloney did his best to sound shocked.

"I said I wouldn't trust Karney."

"You mean the deputy?" Maloney asked, all innocence.

Guild mocked him. " 'You mean the deputy?' Maloney, remember who you're talking to. Guild. The man who brought you in. We spent two days together. Did I ever strike you as dumb?"

"I don't know what you're talking about."

"About bribery, for one thing."

"Bribery?"

"That's right. How much did he offer you?"

"Guild, Christ."

"And he probably threatened you, too, didn't he?"

"No. No, he didn't. I swear."

"You swear."

"I was asleep."

"A man put a rope up there and hung himself and you didn't hear him?"

"I sleep heavy."

49

Guild shook his head. "What did Karney promise you?"

"I told you, Guild."

Then the lockup door opened and Karney was there. He didn't come into the cell block. He just stood there with his rifle in his arms and said, "Sheriff had to go someplace, Guild. He asked me to ask you to leave."

Guild looked at Maloney. "Don't trust him, Maloney. Don't trust him at all."

He walked up to the door and started past Karney.

The deputy leaned into him and said, "You could be charged with assault."

Guild said, "You come and arrest me personally, all right, Karney?"

He left.

The sun came in through the dusty window and fell on the bed where she lay with her eyes wide open and the locket in her fingers and the Peacemaker right there by her side. Ready.

She thought of the man who had raised her and she thought of the woman in her locket, the one she called Ma, and she thought of Earle. Mostly now, she thought of Earle, watching him deal cards, watching him fill in as a barker for the Fat Lady and the Bearded Lady and Katnya from Egypt. She thought of how fine and handsome he looked in his red vest and lacy white shirt and how gentle his hands could be when she took to trembling for no good reason at all during the night. And she thought of how she'd held him on his own bad nights, held him and rocked him and shushed him when he got frightened of his own bad luck or bad tendencies. He'd known jokes fun as flowers, and when it was her birthday (she'd just made one up, March 14) he'd made her feel special as a princess.

They'd had a lot of bad names for Earle but she didn't

give a damn because she knew better, she knew about his curious innocence and how fascinated he'd always been with kittens and the way the moon rose and the spectral sounds you heard in the woods sometimes.

She'd known all these things and cared deeply about all these things the way a sister might care or a mother might care, and she was not going to let Mr. Frank Cord get away with it.

She was not going to let Frank Cord get away with it at all.

Chapter Eight

The next morning they buried Earle Walter Hammond, Jr. on a hill shaggy with spring grass and overlooking a small stream where dogwood and juneberry and wild roses had begun to bloom. The air was tangy with prairie clover, and the breeze was almost chilly, despite the fine day.

Annie would not so much as look at Guild. Not when the priest came and got out his scapular and his holy water and his Bible and laid the body to rest. Not when Guild tugged on his gloves and picked up the shovel and started filling in the dirt. Not when he put the shovel down and looked at the wooden cross and shook his head.

"Guess we're all done here," Ruby Gillespie said.

She put her arm through Annie's.

"You just walk a ways down the hill, all right?" Annie said.

Ruby looked at Guild. They'd both been concerned about the young girl ever since Hammond's death.

"Take Guild with you," Annie said.

Guild nodded. Together he and Ruby went halfway down the long hill and stood by a hardwood. A wild dog roamed by, wary, keeping to the longest part of the grass. Guild built himself a cigarette.

"She's going to need watching," Ruby said.

"I know."

Ruby looked at him closely. "She'll forgive you, Guild."

"I'm not sure I'm worth forgiving."

Ruby started to say something else, but then they saw Annie sink to the ground up on the hill. She embraced the cross. Even from here her moaning was a chilling sound, even lost on the wind.

"You'd better go get her," Guild said.

"No," Ruby said softly. "You go get her."

"You sure?"

Ruby nodded.

He went up the hill and stood by her. She was still slumped over the cross. A yellow butterfly hovered over her head then soared to the blue sky. Twice he put out his hands to take her but he could not bring himself to touch her. He did not want to set her off wailing again.

Finally, gently, he said, "I envy you, Annie."

She didn't move.

"You're lucky to have somebody to love the way you do Earle. And that picture of your Ma."

Slowly her head turned around and she looked at him and said, "You ain't going to let me hate you, are you?"

"What?"

"I'm tryin' as hard as I can to hate you but I can't."

"I'm glad of that, Annie."

She looked back at the cross. Her pinafore was muddy where she'd knelt in the wet earth. "You think he can hear us?"

"Maybe."

"You think he can see us?"

"Maybe."

"I sure hope so," Annie sad. "I sure hope so." She

started crying again, but this time it was soft crying. He put his arms out and took her shoulders and got her to her feet.

She put her face into his chest and the crying came harder now, and purer, and he just listened and swayed slightly in time to the rhythms of her grief. There were birds and more butterflies and a breeze from the stream below and the hazy blue mountains in the distance, and somehow her tears seemed a natural part of it all.

Then he felt her stiffen in his grasp and she pushed away from him.

"That Frank Cord. He needs to die."

Even though her face was still puffy from crying, her eyes were dry. Some of the loveliness was gone from the shape of her face. He saw the hard prairie girl in her. Competent, even cunning.

"Yes, he does," Guild said.

"You going to help me?"

"Yes, I am."

"But you got to make me one promise, mister."

"What's that?"

"You got to let me do it myself when the time comes."

"Kill him yourself, you mean?"

She nodded. "I'm gonna need your help to trap him, mister, but when the time comes—you promise me?"

"I promise you," Guild said.

She put her hands to her face and wiped away the rest of her tears. "There's one other thing."

"What?"

"I don't know that I'll ever be able to forgive you."

"I know."

"Sometimes I'll just think of Earle and I'll get real mad."

He nodded.

"So you try not to hate me, mister, and I'll try not to hate you."

"All right, Annie," he said. He looked at her with great sorrow and again he thought of the six-year-old girl he'd accidentally shot. "All right, Annie, we've made ourselves a bargain."

Then they went back down the hill to where Ruby waited.

On the way back to town, in the buckboard they'd rented from the livery, Annie said, "How we going to do it?"

"Get Frank Cord?" Guild said.

"So you believe me about Frank Cord?" Ruby said.

"For some reason, he wanted Robertson dead and he wanted Earle dead," Guild said.

"Guild's going to help me get him," Annie said, confidently. "But he promised when the time comes, I could do it myself."

Ruby looked over at Guild and shook her head, as if to say now he was the one filling Annie's head with false hopes.

"The first thing I want to do is go to the inquest," Guild said.

"That's going to be interesting," Ruby replied.

"I know. I want to talk to the judge, point out that Baines and Karney let a man into a cell with a belt."

Ruby thought about this. "Hard to tell how that will go. Judge Harnack has started backing away from the Cord family since McKenzie started moving in—he's afraid of winding up on the wrong side. On the other hand, he owes Mason Cord his job."

Guild said, "All we can do is try."

When they reached town, they took the buckboard back to the livery then walked to Ruby's office.

"I think I'll use the Fitch," Ruby said as they moved toward the messy desks.

55

"The Fitch?" Guild asked.

Ruby pointed to a new brown-colored contraption that sat on one corner of a cluttered desk. The typewriter had three rows of keys and four metal braces inside of which you rolled paper.

"My husband, Eugene, always wrote his important editorials on it," Ruby said. "I never was worth a damn with the thing, but I thought I'd give it a try."

Guild put a thick fingertip on one of the keys. He was not an especially mechanical man, but this instrument interested him.

Ruby saw this, typed out his name, LEO GUILD. The machine made a confident clacking sound as she worked.

Guild smiled.

"It's going to be some editorial, let me tell you," Ruby said. She pecked at the keys.

"I could see where this would take you a while to learn, all right," Guild said.

Then Annie said to Guild and Ruby, "Guess I'll go change into my butternuts." They could see she was going to cry again and needed to be alone.

She went out the door. They could hear her going up the stairs that ran alongside the office.

"Take her along with you, Guild, to the inquest and everywhere else," Ruby said. "That way she won't just have to sit around. That was the mistake I made with Eugene. I spent two weeks just smoking his cigars and drinking his whiskey and crying my eyes out."

They spent a few more minutes talking and then Annie was back. Her golden hair was pulled back into a loose bun. There was one other thing, too. In her waist was Earle Hammond's Peacemaker.

Guild knew better than to say anything about it.

"Why don't we go have some food before the inquest?" Guild said.

"I don't know if I'm real hungry," Annie said. The way she touched the Peacemaker, Guild knew she wanted things to happen, and fast.

"Be careful, Annie," Ruby said, but Annie was already out the door and standing on the boardwalk.

Guild paused in the doorway and smiled back at Ruby. "You sure it's a good idea I take her along?"

Ruby smiled back. "An old bastard like you is going to need her energy, Guild. You wait and see."

His father had come here in the first migration, long before there were settlers as such. You could raise wheat and you could raise cattle. You could hunt buffalo and bison and ringnecked pheasant. You could build your home and raise your children the way you wanted them raised. You could stand on a cliff and look for miles at pine and hardwood and aspen and rivers and streams and the ragged mountain chain. This was the Territory, and all it asked for purchase was that you be able to tolerate cholera and influenza and ague and typhoid and scurvy, and that you be able to endure the fact that many of your young ones would die before they reached age five. And it asked that you fight Indians, red men whose women came around after your brothers and uncles were slain and skinned them—as you yourself skinned squirrels or possums—Sioux and Chippewa fierce in their fear and hatred of the white man.

He had come from such a heritage, Mason Cord, the sixty-seven-year-old man who sat in a leather armchair in a den that cost more than most civic buildings in the Territory.

He had come from such a heritage and he had held at bay the notorious forces of Alexander McKenzie, who was the most powerful man in the Territory and the bedfellow of the grain men and the railroads. But now McKenzie had surrounded him, buying up huge parcels of land, putting

57

on those subtle monetary and social payrolls some of the more influential of Mason Cord's old friends, positioning himself to snap with the violence of a viper when age took Mason Cord.

To withstand McKenzie and his money and his force, Cord needed a son who took succor from the blood of the slain, who found wisdom in the brute and uncaring vagaries of the land itself. But Mason Cord's seed had not sown such a one; instead he had received, like a badly flawed gift, his son Frank. Whom McKenzie would crush—if Frank's own foolishness did not bring down the Cord empire first.

"Brandy," Mason Cord snapped.

He had the features of a Roman senator, lost slightly now in jowls and wattles. But the nose and the angry blue eyes spoke of a pride that most men could neither stand up to nor understand.

The Chippewa housemaid, a fleshy woman in a denim dress and beaded headband, had been dusting the mantle. When Cord demanded brandy, she jumped as if somebody had shot her.

She poured him his drink from a green glass decanter with a hammered brass stopper into a genuine Dutch engraved goblet.

Mason Cord's father had been a mountain man who could not read, but Mason Cord had made sure that by the time they put the dirt over *him,* he would have enjoyed more than the old man had.

The maid went to the window and said, "Your son is here, sir."

"Leave," Mason said. He grimaced. He had his foot stretched out on an ottoman. Gout had ravaged his left foot. It was ugly to look at, more ugly to feel.

The maid nodded and left.

The front door opened and sharp steps came across the

58

hardwood vestibule floor and down the hall, and then his son stood in front of him.

Frank had always been too pretty for Mason's tastes. He'd gotten the Roevere looks from his mother's side. There was too much petulance in the eyes and mouth. Womanly petulance.

Mason Cord said, "I want you to tell me exactly what happened last night."

"Can't you say good morning, Father?" Trying a smile women might find fetching.

Frank wore a suede riding jacket and a white shirt and black twill riding pants and black riding boots. His grandfather had caught timber rattlers and gutted them and eaten the innards raw to survive, and here was Frank one generation later looking like an Easterner.

"With this goddamn foot, I'm in no mood for what you like to call the amenities."

Frank smirked and helped himself to the brandy. "Do you think Alexander McKenzie greets people this way?"

"I don't give a good goddamn what Alexander McKenzie does. He can shit his pants and sit around in it all day for all I care. I just want an answer to my question. What happened last night?"

Frank sipped brandy, went over and sat on the edge of a leather couch. The den sparkled in sunlight through mullioned windows. "Harold Robertson got shot."

"What the hell was he doing there?"

For the first time, his son's eyes showed a hint of evasion. "Well, he was working, of course."

"Working at midnight? In a bank?"

"He was our accountant, Father. You seem to forget that. Accountants can work any time of night or day."

Mason Cord eyed his son the way a jeweler would a gem he suspected of being imitation.

"Working? At midnight? You're sure?"

Frank Cord slammed down his drink. "Just what the hell are you accusing me of, Father?"

"I don't know."

"What's that supposed to mean?"

"It means that I don't have any evidence that you've done anything, but that something about this doesn't feel right."

Frank forced a smile. "My God, Father. Can't you give me the credit I've deserved? I've grown up and taken my responsibilities."

"How is Lea?"

"Fine."

"Is she pregnant again?"

Frank flushed. "It appears we'll only have the two girls, Father."

Now it was Mason's turn to slam down his drink. "That comes from your years of whoring. You spent your best juices on harlots."

Frank stood up. "I thought I'd come out and see how you were doing. I can see I caught you in the wrong mood."

Mason Cord's eyes did not leave his son's. "You know what McKenzie's trying to do."

"I know, Father."

"He's buying up every bank in the area. He wants to get a footing here in Danton."

"I know."

"If our bank should fail or falter in any way . . ." He did not finish the thought.

"Everything is fine, Father. It's fine."

He stood there, face boyish except for graying at the temples and lines around his mouth and eyes that almost looked painted on. He would always be a boy, no matter how gray his hair got. He would be buried a boy.

The senior Cord knew now that he had made a mistake

five years ago when he'd put Frank in charge of the bank. But in those days Mason had been pursuing other business interests, and the bank had not been so important. But over the last months the other business interests had failed. Now all they had for their financial foundation was the bank, and if anything was wrong it was too late to do anything about it.

Mason Cord said, "I just hope you haven't done anything foolish, Frank. Because this time I can't get you out of it. And this time it would take me down along with you. You understand?"

Frank said, "Yes, Father, I understand."

His left eye had begun to tic. He departed without another word.

Chapter Nine

When Frank Cord got back to the bank, he discovered immediately he had two problems. One of them he could see sitting in a chair outside his office, and the second of them the fussy clerk Styles brought to him.

Styles, a birdy man who probably wore his green eyeshade to bed, said, "Mrs. Palmer would like to see her money."

"Oh, Christ, Styles, can't you handle it?"

"She insists on having you do it. She says her husband always dealt with the president of the bank and she expects nothing less."

Frank Cord looked around the bank for sight of the little woman. This was an elegant place, heavy with gilt decorations, even on the four teller cages, and rich with flocked wallpaper and pure mahogany furnishings. Expensive reproductions of such masters as Rembrandt and Vermeer were hung every few feet.

Cord's eyes rested on the short, bulky man in the black business suit who sat outside the president's office, drawing on a thick cigar.

Cord's palms began to sweat immediately.

No doubt about who the man represented or why he was here.

An image of the main gambling room in the Timbers filled Frank Cord's mind and he saw himself throw the dice in his crazed double-or-nothing attempt to win back the $25,000 he'd dropped earlier in the evening.

The dice rolled out, tumbling, on the green felt surface.

The people standing around, almost as wrought-up as Frank himself, watched as the dice turned over once and then stopped.

Now his mind filled with a vision of Winters, the stolid, handsome, unlikely owner of the Timbers, who always wore a green silk vest under a pearl gray suit jacket. "I think you'd better come back to my office, Mr. Cord, and we'll make ourselves some arrangements."

That had been six weeks ago. Arrangements had called for the money to be paid in full last week. As it had always been paid in full before. But that had been before grain prices had begun slipping and farmers had started missing payments on their loans.

Frank had been spending the bank's money for years. Now even the bank was running out of money.

"She's waiting, Mr. Cord," Styles said in his testy little way.

"What?"

"Mrs. Palmer."

"Oh. Yes."

"She's over by the vault."

Cord shook his head. "Then let's get it over with."

Styles paused a moment. "May I say something, Mr. Cord?"

"What is it, Styles?"

He tugged on his green eyeshade. "I know we're in mourning here." And with that he indicated the black bunting placed around the bank. "For poor Mr. Robertson, of course. But I really think we should keep a shine on our shoes and a smile in our hearts for the sake of our customers, if nobody else.''

''A shine on our shoes and a smile in our hearts?''

''Yes, that's the favorite saying of the First Fundamentalist Church, where my Evvie and I go.''

''I see.''

''And I think it's a darn good idea.''

''It's great advice,'' Cord said, wanting to smash the prissy little prig in his prissy-little-prig face. A shine on our shoes and a smile in our heart—and Mrs. Palmer on top of it?

They went over to the vault, outside of which waited a tiny lady in a blue gingham dress with a matching bonnet. Her husband, one of the first immigrants in the area, had owned a bakery. He'd been one of those men who'd been so frugal that he'd been able to turn a modest success into the kind of holdings that many more prominent people could only envy.

But Mrs. Palmer and her husband shared one fear, as did many people in the Territory. Banks were always going down, particularly back in the depression of the early sixties, so just to make sure her money was there Mr. Palmer used to come in and ''look'' at his money.

Now Mrs. Palmer carried on that tradition.

''Good day, Mrs. Palmer.''

Cord tried to keep his eyes from drifting over to the man in front of his office. Kendricks, the man's name was. Stories were that he was such a zealous worker for Winters that he'd once cut off the nose of a man who'd tried to fink on a loan, the way some Indian tribes cut off the noses of squaws who'd been unfaithful.

''You look upset today, Mr. Cord. Does my presence here aggravate you?''

Obviously she was challenging him to be rude. It gave

certain local people a great deal of satisfaction to be unpleasant to a member of the Cord family. Made them feel powerful.

"I'm very happy to see you," Cord said.

She smiled—smirked, really. "And I'm very happy to be seeing my money."

He pointed the way to the walk-in vault and then proceeded inward.

The interior of the vault was mostly slots holding metal boxes in which cash, bonds, and some jewelry were kept.

The cash itself was stored in strongboxes for transportation and set in the rear of the large metal cavern.

Cord held his breath when they went inside, wondering if any of the employees, the nosy Mr. Styles for example, had figured out what Cord had been doing lately.

Taking money from the strongboxes and putting it into the slots gave the casual impression of an overflow of greenbacks.

At least Cord hoped that was the impression it gave.

His deception worked for Mrs. Palmer.

"Do you mind?" she said.

"Not at all," he said.

Cord looked over at his clerk. Mr. Styles, it seemed, had a shine on his shoes and a smile in his heart.

She put out a hand and took a stack of greenbacks from one of the slots and started counting it out.

"It just amazes me sometimes," she said. "Nearly everybody in town has money in here." She laughed. "If it was all in one account, somebody would be very rich."

Cord managed a laugh. "Very rich, Mrs. Palmer. Very rich."

She looked the vault over with the eye of a general inspecting troops.

"Well, everything looks to be in order."

"Oh, very much so, Mrs. Palmer."

She smiled. "Do you still have free coffee and cookies in the back for your employees?"

"We most certainly do."

That was another thing. People liked to feel they knew how to get something free from the Cord family. Especially people like Mrs. Palmer.

"Well, I don't suppose you'd try to stop me if I went back and helped myself now, would you?"

"Oh, I certainly wouldn't," Cord said. "I certainly wouldn't, Mrs. Palmer." He had put a shine on his shoes and a smile in his heart.

"Do you suppose I could borrow Mr. Styles here?"

"Of course."

"He's interested in pewter just as much as I am and we have ever so nice conversations. Don't we, Mr. Styles?"

"Oh, we have wonderful conversations, Mrs. Palmer. Wonderful conversations."

Cord nodded good-bye, disgusted by them both, and then turned back to his office.

Kendricks stood up.

He was no more than five-five but he was bull-like and swarthy, and out of the top of his celluloid collar stuck the bristly black hair of a wild animal.

Cord swallowed hard and went back.

"Hello, Kendricks."

Kendricks wasted no time. "This isn't like you, Mr. Cord."

Cord said, "Please don't say anything until we're inside my office with the door closed."

Cord's secretary sat not far away, and already she looked curious about why a man like Kendricks would be calling on her employer.

Inside the closed door, Kendricks said, "You've paid off a lot of money over the past five years. Never any problem, Mr. Cord. Until the last year or so." He dragged on his cigar, exhaled a light breeze of blue smoke. "You owe the boss a lot of money, Mr. Cord."

"I know."

"And he really wants it cleared up right away." He inhaled again. "I don't like talking to you this way, Mr. Cord. We've always had good relations in the past."

"It's going to be a few weeks yet."

Kendricks smiled. He had jagged teeth. You could imagine him rending meat. Raw meat. "Mr. Cord, you're a respectable man. I don't even feel comfortable talking to you. I mean, my father worked in your father's slaughterhouse and here I am trying to give you orders."

Unlike Mrs. Palmer, Kendricks here seemed to be paying him an odd but genuine deference. "This all makes me real uncomfortable, Mr. Cord."

"I'm sorry you're in this position."

"The boss wants his money in full within forty-eight hours, Mr. Cord."

"All of it?" Cord's head snapped up. "The entire debt?"

"I'm afraid so."

"But, my God—"

"He has a little joke. He says 'Mr. Cord is in the banking business, but I'm not.' "

Cord sank down in the chair behind his desk. His office was even more smartly appointed than the rest of the bank. The dagger-shaped letter opener he toyed with was real silver.

Almost to himself, he said, "I'll have to do it, won't I?"

Kendricks nodded.

Cord sat there, and now an image of a magazine cover painting came to him. There was a palm tree and an ocean and a sailboat bending in the wind. The painting was an illustration for a story by Robert Louis Stevenson. Cord had read it when he was ten. He had never forgotten it, never given up the dream of that palm tree and that ocean and that sailboat.

And now the time had come for that dream to be realized.

He thought of the wife for whom he felt no love or passion, of the father he loathed, of the small town full of priggy Mr. Styleses and crude Mrs. Palmers, and he thought of his children who were strangers to him, and to a few local whores who were, oddly, his only intimate friends—and he knew then that it was time.

At last.

The palm tree.

The ocean.

The sailboat.

Cord leaned forward and smiled. "I hope you'll convey my best to your boss."

"Of course."

"Tell him he'll have his money within forty-eight hours."

Tomorrow or the day after there would be a Wells Fargo stage from out in the Territory, loaded with greenbacks for deposit here. . . .

Kendricks stood there with his strange dignity and intelligence and looked honestly relieved that he did not have to use threat or muscle on a man as respectable as Frank Cord.

He put his derby back on his head and said, "I'm going to go have myself a beer, Mr. Cord. I feel much better. Much better."

Cord said good-bye, but vaguely.

A part of him was already on an exotic green island with an exotic brown-skinned woman.

*   *   *

The inquest was held on the second floor of the gray stone city-council building.

This part of a killing did not hold much interest for most people, apparently. No more than ten sat in the pewlike seats that stretched in front of a wide, officious-looking desk. A tall man with an angular head and the pallor of a consumptive sat in the black robes of a judge. Several lawbooks sat on one edge of his desk, an overflow of papers on the other. He had a nod for everybody who came in. He also had a pocketwatch, which he consulted every half minute or so.

To his right was a jury box where four people, two older men and two older women, sat staring at their hands, looking around the room, or watching the door.

To the left, near the door, stood a paunchy man in the khaki uniform of a deputy. The judge, after looking at his watch again, said, "If anything ever started on time in this Territory, I do believe we'd declare it a holiday."

The deputy knew enough to laugh.

Guild and Annie sat in the rear. Annie glared at everybody in the room as if they were personally responsible for Earle's death.

The judge said, "If Baines isn't here in two minutes, I guess we'll just start without him."

Annie whispered to Guild, "She's crying."

Guild leaned toward her. "Who?"

She nodded to a woman about halfway down the row of seats.

There sat a woman in a calico dress and bonnet. She had very white skin and was pretty in a lifeless kind of way.

The woman would sit and stare straight ahead until a sob would convulse her, and then she would take a lacy handkerchief and put it to her face.

"Wonder who she is?" Annie said.

"I don't know, but it might be worth finding out."

69

Baines and Karney came in without ceremony. Baines carried a carpetbag that for some reason looked familiar to Cord. Behind them was a handsome man in a striped shirt and cravat and a tailor-made blue suit. Gray had just begun to streak his black hair. He had dark, imperious eyes and Guild disliked him immediately. He was the man Guild had seen behind the restaurant last night.

"Frank Cord," Annie said. She put her hand on the Peacemaker she held in her waist.

Guild steadied her.

"I'm going to kill him, Guild," she said. "I swear to you I am." She touched her locket. "I swear it on my locket."

If the inquest was all for show, then it was a good show.

Judge Harley Harnack called Baines, Karney, and Frank Cord in turn and questioned them about the events leading up to and including the death of Earle Walter Hammond.

Mostly, it was tedious, so Guild studied some of the photographs on the wall. They depicted various men who had played a major hand in settling the Territory. They all looked like thieves, killers, and town-trashers and they probably had been. They also seemed to have a preference for posing with rifles in their right hands and their left feet on the carcasses of dead animals. There were dead bison and dead buffalo and dead mountain lions and even a dead bull. Apparently, the matador style in the Territory was to plug the goddamn bull with a bullet.

"He's lying," Annie whispered to every other sentence Baines, Karney, and Frank Cord uttered to the judge.

Finally, a little bit exasperated with the repetition, Guild pulled back her blond hair and put his lips to her ear and said, "Annie, why don't you just say 'Everything they say is a lie' and let it go at that."

70

She gave him a funny look. She looked as if she'd been struck. "You mad at me, Guild?"

"No, but you know they're lying and I know they're lying, so you don't have to say it every time."

Then he saw her jerk away from him and her lower lip start to tremble, and he realized that she was still part kid with a kid's raw feelings and he'd just hurt the hell out of them.

He sat there for the rest of the inquest, feeling guilty.

Two hours later, Frank Cord was finishing up his testimony.

The judge said, "So, Mr. Cord, on the way back from dinner with your wife and friends, you noticed a light in the bank and then you went inside and found Mr. Robertson dying."

"Yes." Cord's face tightened and he raised his head and directed his head toward the jury. "We'd been good friends. You could imagine how I felt. He was laid out on the floor and I raised his head and asked him who did it and he said it was Hammond, who we'd both seen around town."

That was when Annie couldn't take it any more.

"He's lying, Judge!" She jumped to her feet and started running down the aisle to the bench. "He owed Earle four thousand dollars from a card game!"

Guild banged his knee hard getting out of the pewlike seat, cursed loud enough to shock a few old ladies, and then started limping down the aisle to grab Annie, who was just now hurtling herself like a missile at Frank Cord.

Guild got her tight enough to restrain her but not tight enough to keep her from kicking, biting, and scratching him in an attempt to get free so she could go for Cord again.

"Who is this young woman?" the judge demanded.

Cord said, with a great degree of smugness, "Hammond's girlfriend."

As soon as he said it, the judge surprised Guild by saying, "Then if she'll calm down, we'll let her take your seat, Mr. Cord, and give testimony."

"What?" Cord snapped.

The judge said mildly, "This is an inquest, Mr. Cord. We're just trying to find out all the facts."

Guild said, "You going to calm down, Annie?"

"Not if Cord keeps sitting there and lying."

Guild got her turned around. He put his hands on her shoulders and talked directly into her face. "This judge is going to give you a chance to speak your piece. You damn well better settle down and take it. You understand me?"

Annie kept her head down and Guild could tell she was still so mad she couldn't get in control of herself.

But then he saw her touch her locket and sigh deeply, and then half a minute later she raised her head and said, "All right."

"I won't hold with any big emotional displays," the judge said. "I've got three daughters and I get enough of them at home. You promise me that, young lady?"

Annie nodded.

So she went up and sat down. Guild sank down in one of the front seats so she'd feel he hadn't deserted her by going to the back.

Annie straightened her shoulders and said, "Frank Cord owed Earle four thousand dollars."

"For a card game?" the judge asked.

"Yes."

Karney stood up. "Your honor."

The judge glanced up. "What is it, Deputy Karney?"

"I'd like to respectfully say that I just don't see what this has got to do with Earle Hammond hanging himself."

The judge shook his narrow head. "As I told Mr. Cord, Karney, we're here to gather facts. That's all."

Karney frowned and sat back down.

Guild met Baines's glances. Baines looked embarrassed by all this.

The judge said, "We'd better back up here for the sake of the jury."

"What, sir?"

"You'd better tell us your name."

"Annie."

"And what was your relationship with the deceased?"

"You mean Earle?"

"Yes, Earle."

She paused. "He was my best friend. He got me a job with the Johnston Brothers."

"The Johnston Brothers?"

"Well, actually there ain't really brothers. There's just the one. Johnston, I mean."

"And what is the Johnston Brothers?"

"A circus."

"I see. Earle got you a job with them, then?"

"Yes."

"What sort of job?"

"I was his assistant in the magic act. I had to put the doves in his hat and line his sleeves with scarves. Things of that nature."

"All right." The judge seemed alternately amused and baffled. "May I ask how old you are?"

"You may, but I ain't sure."

"You're not sure how old you are?"

"Probably nineteen or twenty. The woman who had me left me with this wheelwright. He raised me till a cancer got him, and then I just started . . . well, working at different things, and I never was sure of my age."

Karney said, "Why don't you ask her what 'different things' she worked at, judge?"

Annie flushed and put her head down. "A lot of young girls done it," she said.

73

Guild looked over at Karney, hard enough that the deputy glanced away quickly.

"Tell us about the card game with Mr. Cord."

So she did. How Cord had come into a local saloon one night where Earle was playing, and how Earle had won two thousand dollars from him, and how forty-eight hours later Cord had come back and asked to play blackjack, and how Earle had then won four thousand dollars total.

The judge said, "Did Mr. Cord make any attempt to pay you?"

"No, the night Earle died, we went to the restaurant where Cord was, and Earle got real mad and demanded the money."

"Earle got real mad?"

Annie shrugged. "We all have failings. One of them was his temper, I guess."

Guild just sort of shook his head. She was making a hell of a case for Frank Cord.

"Did Earle go to the bank that night, Annie?"

"I guess so."

"You weren't with him?"

"No, I just got mad, how he was actin' and all."

"How was he acting?"

"Oh, drunk and angry and—"

"Do you think he could have gone to the bank and tried to rob it the way Mr. Cord said?"

"I don't think so. He was too drunk to do anything but sort of wander around."

Karney said, "I'd like to say something here, your honor."

"All right."

"Frank Cord isn't denying that there was a card game and that he lost money."

"He isn't?"

"No. But that isn't the whole story."

"Then what is the whole story, Mr. Karney?"

From the table, Karney picked up the carpetbag. He opened it and took something out.

He showed the jury a deck of playing cards.

"Do you care to tell me what those are?"

"Poker cards, your honor."

"I mean, do you care to explain their relevance here?"

"They were Earle Hammond's cards."

"May I see them?"

Karney nodded and brought them forward.

"Open the deck, your Honor."

The deck was still sealed.

The Judge opened them up and took out the cards.

At first he didn't seem to find anything amiss.

Karney said, "Look carefully at the edge of some of the cards, Your Honor."

The judge complied and then he said, "I'll be dogged."

"Marked cards, Your Honor. Now open the fresh box."

Which the judge did. He said, again, "I'll be dogged."

"They're the type of cards that professional gamblers—dishonest professional gamblers—can buy already marked. There's a whole system so that they can tell at anytime what their opponents are holding."

"Did you know about this, young lady?" the judge said. He sounded very, very angry.

In a voice that scarcely anybody could hear, Annie said, "That was another one of Earle's failings. He wasn't a real honest card player."

"So you're saying he cheated Mr. Cord?"

"Just 'cause he was a cheat didn't mean he was a killer," Annie cried.

But whatever sympathy she'd managed to get from the judge was gone now.

There were a few more exchanges between the judge and Karney, and Guild tried to bring up the point about

Hammond being allowed to have a belt in his jail cell. Then the strange woman in calico began crying again, and the judge banged his gavel and said, "I don't see any real need to carry these proceedings any further."

And that was it as far as the judge was concerned.

Within five minutes the jury had found that there was no reason in the world to look any further into the sordid existence of one Earle Walter Hammond. He had hanged himself in the local jail and he had, perhaps, done himself and the entire Territory a favor.

The judge brought his gavel down again and the proceedings were finished.

Annie sat silently in the chair next to the judge's bench long after judge, jury, and spectators had left, all except for one.

The woman in calico.

Like Annie, she looked stunned by the proceedings. The guard peeked back in and said, "Would you like somebody to walk you home, Mrs. Robertson?"

After he knew who she was, Guild watched her more carefully. Why would she come to the inquest? What would draw her here?

Guild got very curious and then he heard a thunder of heavy objects hitting the floor behind him.

He whirled around and saw that Annie had shoved all of the judge's lawbooks to the floor.

"I didn't do it right, did I, Guild?" she shouted.

Guild went up to her and took her by the shoulders, and she came into his arms.

"It wouldn't have mattered," Guild said. "No matter what you testified, they had those marked cards and that was bound to turn the jury. It made Earle look bad so they didn't much care one way or another what had happened to him."

She pulled away from him, angry now. "Maybe he

wasn't real honest or anything, but he never deserted me, Guild. He never deserted me."

"I know," Guild said, looking at the lost child she was. "I know." Then he nodded to the door. "But now we've got to go see somebody."

"Who?"

"Mrs. Robertson."

"Why?"

He slid his arm around her. "Come on and I'll tell you over a glass of beer."

Chapter Ten

They were no more than three steps into the saloon when Guild noticed a most unlikely man standing at the bar sipping sour mash from a shot glass and chasing it with a nickel schooner of beer.

A pudgy man in a plain suit.

A man named Maloney.

A man who was supposed to be in jail.

Guild stood at the opposite end of the bar with its long brass footrail and evenly spaced brass spitoons. He looked up at the fancy hanging lamps and then he looked along the six booths where food was served and then he looked back at Maloney.

By now the other man had noticed Guild, too, though he was pretending very hard he hadn't.

Guild, his face pulled tight with anger, went straight up to Maloney and said, "Hope you're enjoying that whiskey, Maloney."

Maloney, obviously afraid at the anger he sensed in Guild, turned and said, "Why wouldn't I?"

"Because it's got blood in it. Earle Hammond's blood."

Maloney knew better than to antagonize Guild further.

He set down his drink and said to the bartender, "Guess I'll go have myself a stroll."

By now the rest of the saloon was watching Guild carefully. A few were even anxiously glancing at the EXIT door in case the man named Guild opened fire, which he looked perfectly capable of.

Maloney put his head down, as if he were trying to will Guild out of existence, and then took his first tentative steps toward the front door.

Guild grabbed him and said, "I'm going with you, Maloney, on your walk. We're going to have a talk."

Annie ran ahead to the batwing doors and held one of them back so Guild could shove Maloney through it.

Maloney went head first, tripped on the doorframe, and then went sprawling out onto the boardwalk.

It was getting on to suppertime. Proper ladies passing by on their way home walked wide of Maloney, as if he were diseased or something. The driver of a mud wagon grinned as he drove by, apparently assuming that Maloney was drunk. "Wish I was feelin' as good as you are!" the driver shouted.

"Get up, you sonofabitch," Guild said.

Annie surprised him by grabbing his arm and saying, "God, Guild, go a little easy on him."

"He knows what happened and he won't tell us."

Maloney put out a hand to be helped up. Guild spat on the boardwalk next to him.

Annie went over and helped him up. "Why don't you help us, Mr. Maloney? You're not like Cord. You're just like me and Guild, just regular folks."

Maloney kept his eyes from her.

Guild, still wanting to smash the man's face in, instead grabbed him by the collar of his jacket and said, "We're taking him over to Ruby's."

For the first time, Maloney resisted. He tried to jerk

away from Guild's grasp. "They put me free, Guild, and there ain't a damn thing you can do about it."

"How'd they put you free? Your face is on that WANTED poster.

"Sheriff Baines said as far as he's concerned, it's a case of mistaken identity."

This time, Guild couldn't stop himself. He brought his right fist up and cracked Maloney directly on the chin.

"God, Guild," Annie said, rushing to the older man as he started to sink to the ground from the punch.

Guild pushed her out of the way.

He went over and got Maloney by his lapels and got him upright on his feet again.

Then he shoved him down the boardwalk and ordered him to start walking.

"Looks like you got hit with a crowbar," Ruby said when they'd gotten Maloney to sit down in a straight-back chair in the one-room *Chronicle* office.

"No," Annie said. "Guild hit him with his fist—and he shouldn't have, either."

For some reason Guild could not understand, Annie was very protective of Maloney, even though the plaid-suited man probably held the key to exposing the men who'd murdered Earle.

The blow had stunned Maloney enough that he was only now coming to full consciousness.

He looked around the office, obviously unable to figure out where he was, and then he looked at Ruby and something changed in his face.

Guild was aware of it and Annie saw it, too, because a smile broke on her face.

Guild had to admit to himself that it was good to see some kind of pleasure take her, if only momentarily.

With almost comic ceremony, Maloney doffed his dusty derby and said, "Good evening, ma'am."

Ruby grinned. "And good evening to you."

"My name's Maloney."

"And mine's Gillespie."

"For Christ's sake, Ruby," Guild said.

The gray-haired woman came abruptly to her senses, looking like a teenage girl who'd been caught flirting with the neighbor boy.

She frowned at Maloney. "You seem to have made my friend Guild pretty mad."

"He hit me."

"I'll say he did," Ruby said. "Why don't we get a cold rag and you can hold it against the bruise."

"No!" Guild said.

The other three of them froze as Guild moved to the table where they all sat.

"Why the hell are you and Annie taking this man's part?" Guild said.

Ruby said, "I guess because he looks sort of defenseless."

"And that's just what I am," Maloney said to Guild. "Defenseless. I don't have no money. I don't have no home. I don't have nothing." Maloney knew an opening when he saw it, and he took it.

Guild said, "A ham actor would be ashamed for saying those words, Maloney."

"Well, they're the truth, Guild. They're the honest to God truth." Maloney touched his chin for emphasis. His eyes smarted when he did so.

"They took you out, didn't they, Maloney, and then they hung him?"

Maloney put his head down.

Guild was tired of him, of this whole town, of this whole setup.

"I asked you a question, Maloney."

His voice was harsh in the silence.

Then he lost control of his temper again and jumped for Maloney and got him by the collar and hurled him up and into the wall.

Guild was going to wade into him and had already started swinging, but Ruby and Annie got in front of him and held him off.

"Have you gone crazy?" Ruby screamed. "Now, God damn you, Guild, you calm down—you hear me?—you calm down!"

So Guild stood there and let the anger go through him until his breathing became regular and his head did not feel quite so buzzy.

When it appeared she could handle him better, Ruby said, "You come outside with me a minute, Guild."

"What?"

"You heard me. I said come outside."

Guild looked over at Annie, who was helping Maloney to his feet. She wasn't paying any attention to Guild whatsoever and he felt, incredibly, slighted.

"Outside," Ruby Gillespie said. She might have been talking to an eight-year-old.

Out on the boardwalk, you could smell the spring day dying, the gardenia breeze and the scent of new grass. A quarter-moon hung in the sky again.

"Let me tell you something about myself," Ruby said. She was a foot and a half shorter, but she didn't seem to have any fear whatsoever about jabbing Guild in the chest for emphasis. "What you did back in there is animal behavior. The Good Lord doesn't sanction it and neither do I."

The way he bowed his head, unable to speak, Guild felt as gutless as Maloney.

"Now that's a man who's had misery and failure in his life, and you can see it in his eyes and hear it in his voice.

And now he's got fear, too—fear that he's letting you down, and fear that Cord and his men will kill him if he doesn't let you down. He deserves better than that, and I'm damn well going to give it to him." By the time she'd finished speaking, she was as wild-eyed as Guild himself had been. "He can't help it—he's a fearful man, Guild. The world is a fearful place. Now we're going back in there and we're going to treat him with some decency and some dignity. He's in sore need of those things."

"He can help us hang Cord," Guild said. Then, "Anyway, why do you hold him so special, a sensible woman like you?"

"Just 'cause I've got gray in my hair and liver spots on my hand doesn't mean I'm a matron, Guild." She looked behind him a moment, at some truth only she could see. "He reminds me of my husband—damned if he doesn't."

Guild shook his head, sighed.

She looked at him. "Did you ever think kindness might encourage him to honesty before violence will?" She pointed her finger at him. "You're just as weak as he is, Guild. The only difference is, you don't know it. But then, most men don't." She put her arm on his and said, "Now I want you to go back in there and shake his hand and apologize."

"What?"

"Just what I said. I want you to go back in there and apologize."

"For what?"

"For being a stupid brute."

"The hell."

"The hell yourself, Guild. Now you get back in there."

And just as she'd led him out the door, Ruby Gillespie led him back in the door and marched him over to the table where Maloney sat, Annie at his side.

"Now tell him," Ruby said.

Maloney kept his head down.

"No," Guild said.

Ruby said, "Guild, do you know how miserable I can make your life? If Eugene was still alive he'd tell you. Plenty miserable, believe me. Now tell him."

"Shit," Guild said.

But he whispered it.

"Mr. Maloney?"

Slowly, Maloney looked up.

"Guild here has something he wants to say," Ruby said. She nodded to Guild.

Guild shook his head and said, "She wants me to apologize."

Ruby said, "You don't apologize because somebody wants you to, Guild. You apologize because *you* want to. Because you acted like a stupid asinine animal. Now stand up straight and open your mouth good and wide and make your apology, and then I'll make us all some dinner."

So Guild said it—what choice did he have with Ruby on him?—with his shoulders thrown back and his voice big and loud and his hand out in a gesture of friendship. "I got a little carried away there, Maloney, and I'm sorry."

Maloney looked afraid to take Guild's hand, as if it might be a trick, but finally he did. He said, "You really sorry, Guild?"

Ruby said, "I wouldn't push your luck, Mr. Maloney."

"No," Maloney said, "no, I guess I better not push my luck, should I?"

Ruby grinned and came up and slapped Guild on the shoulder, and then she set about making them a meal of braised beef and corn muffins and apple sauce and blueberry wine. She even found half a leftover rhubarb pie.

Chapter Eleven

Frank Cord stood over the bed of his sleeping five-year-old daughter and wished he felt what he suspected other fathers felt when they looked at their children.

But he didn't and never had.

During an argument he'd once had with his wife, Lea, she'd accused him of "being bored when he wasn't gambling and carousing with whores," and deny it as he might, there'd been truth in her words.

Periodically, especially during the times his father threatened to disinherit him, Cord had tried to play the role of happy husband but it never lasted long, and it was never very good. The truth was, he'd lost his passion for his proper, "cultured" wife shortly after he'd gotten her pregnant five months before their marriage, and his two daughters could not hold his attention for much longer than half an hour at a time. After a few weeks of chastened living, he'd become like a man who wanted a drink but had been denied it—irritable and crazed, like something caged. Then he'd slip back to his old ways, a card game here, a whore there, and finally he'd be spending more and more time away from home, eventually winding up at the Timbers where cards and whores were in ample supply.

His daughter rubbed her face and then rolled over on her side. For a stray moment he felt a tenderness for her, for her looks, really, the regal Swedish looks of her mother. He also felt guilt for what he would do within the next forty-eight hours. Once he'd gone, there would be no way he could ever return. She and her sister would grow to be women without ever knowing their father. They would be financially secure because Lea's father was wealthy—but they would be raised without a man unless Lea married again.

He sighed, feeling old beyond his years, not even the prospect of brown-skinned women and a trunk full of money able to buoy him.

From the doorway of the shadowed room, Lea said, "She's beautiful, isn't she?"

"Beautiful."

"We're lucky to have one blonde and one brunette."

"Yes."

"That way they each have their own special beauty."

"Yes."

There was a pause. He could sense her tension. "Do you know how long it's been?"

"I'm afraid I don't know what you're talking about, Lea."

He had yet to turn around. Face her.

"Of course you know." A pause again. "It's been nearly four months."

"I'm sorry."

"It's not even that I always enjoy it so much. It's just that I know what it signifies."

"We've been getting along very well."

"You're with your whores again."

He glanced over at the other bed now. At the dark-haired daughter. She had a doll sleeping next to her. He smiled. Reached down and touched her shoulder. He could not believe what he felt suddenly—the tears forming in his eyes, some profound regret cutting even deeper than his lusts.

He turned back to Lea and said, still floating on some kind of sentiment that almost rocked him, "I need to tell you something."

"What?"

"That I appreciate all the things you've done for me in our marriage."

Lea, in light, glowed in her white lacy dinner dress, her open features clean and strong.

"It's more than your whores this time, isn't it?" she said as he came to her.

"I can deal with it."

"I wish I could describe what I see in your face, Frank. I don't think you know how bad you look." She touched his face gently. "I'm afraid for you. For us."

"I'll be all right." He put his hand over hers. He said, "I would like to spend time with you tonight." He let his eyes move down the hall to the master bedroom. Their home was a smaller version of the mansion in which his father lived.

Lea said, "Frank, won't you let me help you? I'm strong, Frank."

He wished he felt the pure unalloyed desire for her he knew with his fifteen-year-old perfumed sluts. But he felt only a deadening gratitude.

"I can be strong for us, Frank. Please tell me what's wrong."

He thought of her gentleness, of her liking for Chopin and Shakespeare and watercolors. She liked to walk in the woods and find leaves of interesting shape and coloration, and sit on their upstairs porch and smell the vines after a rainstorm. She understood and enjoyed all the things that mattered, and he understood none of them.

"Please let me help you, Frank," she said.

And he almost told her.

All of it.

What had happened.

And how bad it was.

How bad it really was.

For the first time ever in their marriage, Frank Cord buried his head in his wife's neck and began to cry.

They ate in one of the upstairs rooms and the dinner was fine and festive and Guild even managed, with the help of two water glasses of wine and several warning looks from Ruby Gillespie, to relax.

The women continued doting on Maloney, giving him extras, listening attentively to his expansive version of his life story, told, as he leaned back in a chair with one of Guild's cigars in his mouth, like a circus barker announcing a special attraction.

According to Maloney, his father had trekked from New Hampshire to Ohio Territory after the collapse of the New York banks in 1837, the fault of President Andrew Jackson's reckless fiscal policies and massive debt. Father and son alike worked as bakers until talk of gold in California in 1848, when they immediately hit the Oregon trail with a cart and two oxen. But their experience was not unlike that of many others along the trail—they found no gold in California. Just starvation and disease and violence. Maloney's father died when two drunken gold-panners crushed his skull with a rock only to discover that the old man had no money. Eventually, Maloney himself drifted back to the Territory, where he held a succession of jobs.

All this was fine listening and probably true. The parts

that bothered Guild were the interwoven tales of fighting off Indians and meeting shootists such as Wild Bill Hickock and the Earp brothers and the James Gang. At one point, caught up in his own bull-slinging, Maloney even had Jesse James fighting a Comanche with knives.

Obviously Ruby and Annie knew these tales were lies— Annie sort of smiled at Guild whenever Maloney told an especially big whopper, and Ruby winked at Guild when Maloney mentioned Jesse James and Comanches—but nonetheless they listened like little girls to an uncle just back from the wilds.

Around this time, Guild began to lose interest and he thought again of Mrs. Robertson and how strange it was she'd come to the inquest at all. He also kept thinking of how she'd exploded into little bursts of tears. She was a troubled woman, understandable enough now that she'd lost a husband, but he sensed another source of trouble, too.

Finally, when he could slip a word into the conversation, he said, "Anybody mind if I go for a walk?"

Everybody stared at him.

"We're having a nice, pleasant evening here," Ruby said.

"I know," Guild said, "but there's something I need to do."

As soon as he said that, Annie tensed in her chair. "Where you going, Guild?"

"Well," he said. He hadn't really planned on taking her along.

"Well, what?" she demanded.

"I kind of thought I might go over and see Mrs. Robertson."

"And you weren't going to take me with you? I thought we were partners."

He let out a long sigh. "Yeah, I guess we are."

"Then I can go along?"

"I guess."

"You guess?"

"Sure you can go along."

"That's a damn sight better."

"Then let's go."

Annie hopped up and leaned over to Ruby and kissed her on the cheek and said, "This dinner's been great, Ruby."

"It certainly has been," Maloney said, still expansive, ashing his cigar on his dinner plate.

Now Guild stood up. To Ruby he said, "Can I talk to you a minute?"

She nodded and got up herself. "Be right back," she said to Annie and Maloney.

When they were down the hall, Guild said, "You going to work on him?"

She glared at him. "I am working on him, Guild. With good food and kindness."

"Fine," he said, "then by the time we get back, I expect he'll be willing to go with me to the judge and tell him what really happened the other night in jail."

Ruby smiled. "I've got one more weapon left, Guild."

"What's that?"

"I've got this special sachet. Maloney looks like a man who'd be susceptible to sachet."

"He'd also be susceptible to getting his jaw broken."

She laughed. "You just watch how my sachet works, Guild. You just watch."

They went back into the room, and he got Annie, and they went out into the spring night. Main Street was filled with roistering workers and saloon denizens, and a few more proper people headed to the opera house.

They stopped at the pharmacy where a man with muttonchops and a white coat told them where they'd find the Robertson house.

"What are you going to ask her?" Annie said.

"I'm not sure yet. We'll just have to see what happens."

"You were just pretending you weren't having a good time back there at Ruby's, weren't you?"

"I don't like the idea of feeding a man who won't help us."

"He's just scared is all."

Guild shook his head and looked up at the street sign and saw the small white Robertson house. Lamps glowed in the windows. A white picket fence glowed in the moonlight.

"Maybe she won't even talk to us," Annie said.

"Maybe she won't. But I guess we're going to find out one way or another."

They started across the sandy street.

They had gotten halfway to the house when rifle fire cracked through the night, shattering the front window of the Robertson house.

Inside a woman screamed and children began crying.

Guild instinctively pushed Annie to the ground, jerked out his own weapon and began firing from the ground in the approximate vicinity of the rifle volleys.

Somebody else was interested in Mrs. Robertson.

Very interested in Mrs. Robertson.

Chapter Twelve

Guild took Annie's shoulder and pulled her along as he duck-walked to an elm tree, which offered at least partial protection from the rifleman.

Then he sent more bullets in the direction of the dark house from across the street. As moonlight was the only illumination, he could only guess where the gunman waited.

Mrs. Robertson, trying to calm her children, went through the rooms, putting out the lamps. Soon her house was as dark as the one across the street. She would be safe at least temporarily.

"I'm going to circle wide and try to get in that house across the street," Guild said.

"I'm going with you."

"No, you're not."

"God damn you, Guild, we're partners."

"You're talking so loud you're giving him an easy target."

She sulked. "You promised."

"I didn't promise this part of it."

"All or nothing."

"That's not how I look at it."

92

"Maybe that's the man who killed Earle."

Guild pulled her so close their faces were almost touching. He tried to deny what he felt in that instant but he couldn't. Unable to stop himself, he put his lips to hers very gently. She still tasted of the blueberry wine. He touched her golden hair and it was as if his fingers ignited. He had been so lonely so long and now she was here, and it was both the most wonderful and the most terrible thing that had ever happened to him.

"God, Guild," she said, when they parted. "I don't know if you should have done that. Now I'm just so doggone confused. I really am."

Rather than face the situation he'd created here, he eased his way up behind the tree and said, "You just stay behind this tree and don't move. You hear me?"

Without giving her a chance to object, he ran wide down the street. The rifleman saw him. Bullets tore into trees, dug up dirt, missed Guild by inches.

He was sweaty and out of breath as he sank to the ground behind an oak. He needed to run across the street then sneak up on the back of the house. He did not want to think about what could go wrong because if he thought long he would be pinned down here forever.

He bolted, racing across the street, weaving in such a way that the rifleman would have a difficult time catching him.

He made it to the other side of the broad avenue and dove behind a mulberry bush. The berries smelled sweet-sour as he lay there getting his breath back.

Then he was up moving again. He ran parallel to a windbreak of hardwoods to the alley that would lead him to the rifleman's position.

He stopped halfway there to reload his weapon again, then he started his inch-by-inch progress up to the house.

*　　*　　*

Baines had spent the last ten years of his life talking to dead people. By now it seemed a perfectly natural thing to do.

Presently, he sat in his rented room in a boardinghouse near the bluffs near the north edge of town. There was no lamplight, just the glow of his pipe as he sat there rocking back and forth in the carved oak rocker he had made his wife for her fifty-second birthday.

His wife was one of the dead people he spoke to. He had, in fact, just been speaking to her.

I used to be an honorable man, he said. *But no longer. I guess it doesn't make any difference anymore, you gone and all.*

He sat there and listened to the noise the rocker made and smelled the cherry smell of his pipe and watched the way leaf shadows played on the wall of his room.

I used to be an honorable man.

And true, he had been. Which is not to say he had not, in his official capacity as sheriff, taken certain amounts of money from wealthy people to overlook the antics of a son or the special treatment of a friend.

But nobody would ever claim that lawmen in the Territory were angels. Angels could not handle the violence or the long hours or the abuse of citizens. So Territory lawmen had to be measured by degrees of honor, by degrees of honesty. And by that measure, as he'd just finished telling his dead wife, Baines was in fact an honorable man.

At least he used to be.

Before he came to Danton and started to do favors for Frank Cord. Exactly the sort of favors he'd sworn he'd never do. Frank had a bad temper and what he did to whores was . . . Baines had agreed to help Frank out once. Then the second time it had come easier, selling himself this way. Then the third time, when it involved running a gambler out of town whom Frank had owed money . . .

He rocked and he smoked and he talked to dead people. To his brother who'd been killed wearing the Gray in the Perrysville campaign. To his daughter who'd been kicked by a cow and died ten days later at age eight (had his wife ever really gotten over that?). And to a sister who'd perished at age twenty in an outbreak of anthrax.

He not only talked to them, he asked questions.

What he was deciding to do, of course, was to help Guild, to find out what happened at the jail last night, even if it meant displeasing Frank Cord.

But he always asked his dead people for permission first. For anything important, anyway.

Nobody knew him as well as these folks.

Nobody cared as much for him.

So he sent his voice across the void and in no time, he started receiving answers.

I don't much like the way you've been acting anyway, his wife said.

Me, either, Pa, his daughter told him.

So he sat there and thought about it.

What he'd done over the past few years.

How he might extricate himself from Frank Cord's grasp.

It was time.

Past time.

As his dead ones told him.

He was sitting there and rocking and smoking and talking to his dead people when he heard the rifle shots.

In a town the size of Danton such a noise carried far and clear on the soft night air.

And in the sound of it—the cracking harshness of it—he knew that his life here had begun to unravel.

I am an honorable man.

It was time he started acting like one again.

He got up, a splendid-looking man despite the belly and the jowls, a man ham actors should and often did envy, and got his own Winchester from the corner and decided to go see what the rifle shots were all about.

What they were really all about. And not just what Frank Cord might say they were about.

Then he picked up his vest with the brass star on it and the gunbelt containing the .44.

Thank you, he said to his dead ones.

He got his .44 on straight and then he went out.

Guild dove behind a hedge in back of the house just as the rifleman opened fire again.

He was held down for five minutes before he could move. All he could hope for was that Annie didn't do anything stupid, that she stayed behind the tree.

The sound of an owl, the smell of wet grass, the nimbus around the quarter-moon.

He crouched and waited.

Then it was time to move again and he knew there was only one way in and he would have to risk everything to do it.

He stood up from behind the hedge and fired three shots into the window where the rifleman stood.

Then he started running.

Guild's shots made the rifleman cautious enough that Guild was able to run across most of the back yard before the sniper started shooting again.

Guild got the back door open just as the man quit firing. He hoped that the noise of the screen door opening was lost in the volley.

He edged inside, smelled pepper, maple syrup, paprika in the kitchen; a lamp wick and cigar smoke in the living room.

He stood at the base of the stairway leading up to the second story window where the rifleman waited.

Guild stopped to load his gun.

Then, pressing himself flat against the side of the doorway, he picked up a straight-back chair and hurled it into the living room, smashing a lamp.

The rifleman reacted just as Guild had hoped.

He came running down the stairs, slowing up only when he reached the first floor landing.

Guild could hear the man's ragged breathing, smell the sweat on him.

The man, not a smart man, jumped through the doorway and landed on his feet, angling his Remington around in a circle.

Guild moved from the shadows, a piece of moonlight exposing his face, and the man fired instantly.

Guild fired back.

The man screamed and the sound was huge in the well-appointed house.

"Gut-shot," the man moaned, "gut-shot."

He rolled around on the hardwood floor in an ever-thickening puddle of his own blood.

Guild knelt down to the man, his knees cracking as he did so, and said, "Why were you shooting at Mrs. Robertson, Karney?"

But Karney, dying, could only shout at the darkness, "Ma, Ma! Help me, Ma!"

"Shit," Guild said.

Karney wasn't going to be any use to him at all.

Chapter Thirteen

Guild was just leaving the house when he heard the front door squeak open. All he could think of was that Karney had had somebody with him. Karney's dying cries still in his mind, Guild drew his weapon and got ready for another shoot-out.

Then Annie said, "Guild? Guild, are you in there?"

"Christ," Guild said and yanked the door the rest of the way open.

She looked up at him and said, "What're you so mad about?"

"Never come through a door like that, Annie. Not when there's the possibility of trouble."

"Well, I'm sorry," she said, angry.

He put his hand out and touched her shoulder. "I just worry about you is all. That's the only reason I spoke that way."

"Ruby's right. You've got to get a better hold on that temper of yours."

"Look who's talking."

"I have a bad temper?" she said, getting mad again. "I have a bad temper?"

He said, "Karney's in there. Dead."

"Karney? Why would he want to shoot at Mrs. Robertson?"

Guild nodded across the street. "Why don't we go over and find out?"

Twenty minutes later, Baines had all the lamps lit in the downstairs of the house where his deputy had been killed. Doctor Smythe, a slight, balding man who seemed to have had his black bag sewn to his right hand, knelt next to the corpse and said, "Gut shot. Probably didn't take him long to die."

Baines looked around. This was a nice home with furnishings bought in Yankton and other appointments that came all the way from the East. A couple named Harcourt lived here. He wholesaled fur and obviously made a damn good living at it. At the moment the Harcourts were in Kansas visiting a sick relative. Karney had known this. Baines wondered what the hell his deputy had been doing here.

Doctor Smythe said, "Do the Harcourts have a telephone? We should call the mortuary."

"No, but the Bryces do. About a quarter mile from here."

"Good night for a walk. Why don't you let me do it?"

Smythe, bag in hand (did he think Baines would steal it?) strolled out into the night, nodding good-bye.

Baines went back to looking around.

Upstairs, beneath one of the bedroom window frames, he found a dozen spent cartridges. The air stank of cordite. He knelt down and looked out to see what Karney could possibly have been aiming at.

Across the street was the Robertson house. Nothing else. There was, in fact, nothing else out here on this western edge of town. The foothills began here and the piney forests.

If Karney had been firing at something, then his only possible target would have been the Robertson house—

Downstairs he heard footsteps.

Taking out his Colt, he worked his way to the first floor. He was shaking. He was too old for this. Just as he had once been a man of honor, just so had he been a young man and a brave man. But things happened and time passed and you found yourself the way he was now— shaking, sweaty, stomach a painful ruin.

A big man stood with his back to Baines, peering down at the corpse.

At first Baines didn't recognize him, and then realizing who it was, he said, "I hope to hell you didn't do this, Guild."

Guild turned and looked at him. "He didn't leave me a hell of a lot of choice."

"What were you doing out here?"

Guild eyed him coldly. "You thinking of taking me in?"

"I'm trying to find out what the hell happened here. I seem to remember something about me being a lawman."

Guild sighed. "I saw Mrs. Robertson at the inquest. Annie and me came out here to talk to her. But when we got here, somebody was emptying a rifle into her front window from here."

"Karney?"

"Yep."

"Sonofabitch."

Guild decided to ease the moment. "Maybe if I keep talking, I can shame you into doing the right thing."

"I don't know what's going on, either."

"Why don't you ask Frank?"

"Maybe it's time I did." He looked down at Karney. "It's always nice to be able to say a little something good over a dead man."

"Can you think of anything?"

"Not offhand."

Guild laughed. "He was probably nice to his mother."

"Actually, he wasn't. She used to bring cookies by the jail for him and he always got embarrassed."

"That's enough to embarrass anybody."

Baines smiled. "They were good cookies."

Guild looked at him. "What're you going to do, Baines?"

"Go see Cord, I guess."

"Why don't you stop by and have a whiskey first."

Baines said, "That's not a bad idea." He looked back down at Karney. "Not a bad idea at all."

Forty-five minutes later, Baines had had himself two whiskeys. He pushed open the door to the sheriff's office and said to the man behind the desk, "Your cousin's dead."

"What the hell are you talking about?" Frank Cord said.

"Just what I said."

Cord rose so abruptly, he almost brought the desk with him. "Who shot him?"

"Guild."

"That goddamn bounty hunter?"

"Yes."

"Jesus Christ," Frank Cord said, rubbing at his face. "Karney. Dead."

Baines, whiskey-brave, said, "We need to talk."

Cord's gaze became a glare. "I don't like the tone of voice I'm hearing."

"Karney was shooting at the Robertson widow. Trying to scare her, from what I can see. I want to know why."

"How the hell would I know."

"That's not a good enough answer, Cord."

"Oh, it isn't, is it? Since when do I have to answer to some fat ass, over-the-hill lawman?"

"Since now."

"I can smell the whiskey from here. You're drunk."

"Things are getting past your control, Cord."

"They are, are they?"

"Yes, they are."

Cord took out a cigar, bit off the end, spat the tip into the wastebasket.

"I want your badge."

"I'm way ahead of you."

Over his second whiskey, Baines had removed his brass star. He threw it on the desk top.

"You've made a stupid decision, Baines. You could have had it easy here."

Baines stared at him. "You don't seem to understand, Frank. The easy days are over. For both of us."

He nodded good-bye and left.

Twenty minutes earlier, when Guild and Annie had gone over to the Robertsons, the widow had greeted them at the front door with a Cook carbine that was almost more than she could hold and point.

"He's dead," Guild said.

"Who's dead?"

"Karney. The local deputy."

She looked shocked. "Karney was shooting at us?"

Guild nodded.

Then a curious understanding shone in her eyes, as if

she had just realized something that should have been obvious to her all along.

Annie said, "What is it, Mrs. Robertson?"

The widow shook her head, dropped her eyes.

Behind her, a boy of ten or so turned up the light in a lamp, revealing a living room of modest money but pleasant taste. A small fireplace warmed the room. The overstuffed furnishings looked comfortable.

"I'd like to talk to you," Guild said.

"I don't have anything to say to you."

"Please, Mrs. Robertson. At the inquest today—"

"I shouldn't have gone."

"But you did go, and I think I know why."

She glared at him, the loss of her husband and her fear at having been shot at giving her eyes a glazed fury. "You don't know anything about what's going on here."

"Then please let us come in so we can talk."

Annie said, "Earle didn't kill your husband, Mrs. Robertson. He swore to me on something very sacred that he didn't, and he never would have done that if he wasn't telling the truth."

The widow looked at Annie as if the girl might be crazed. Then a frailty overtook her and the Cook appeared way too big in her hands and her shoulders slumped. She seemed twenty years older.

Guild said, "If Karney had wanted to kill you, he could have. He was firing warning shots. I need you to tell me why he'd do something like that, Mrs. Robertson."

"I don't want to talk," she said. Guild could scarcely hear her. The insects on the night were louder than this worn woman. "I don't want to talk," she said.

But she didn't stop him as he eased his way over the threshold and didn't stop him as he guided her to the sofa and didn't stop him as he said to her boy, "Why don't you fix your ma some tea?"

103

And she didn't stop him when he sat down next to her and slid his arm around her, and she just let it all come out in tears and mutters and anger and fear.

Finally, after she'd had some of the tea her boy had fixed her, she started telling them some things about her husband's relationship with Frank Cord.

Chapter Fourteen

Even as a small boy, Kendricks had been fascinated by hangings. Official ones. With all the grim pageantry. Watching a lynching wasn't the same. It was over with too fast and there was no ceremony. There was something about the sound of the nails being pounded into two-by-fours to build the gallows. Something about watching the officials try out the trapdoor again and again. Something about watching the hangman ascend the stairs. Something about watching the victim look real humble and almost dazed right there at the last, just as the minister or priest said a prayer with him. Something about watching the noose being adjusted just so. Something about watching the black hood being dropped over the man's face. Something about watching how the man just kind of dangled there gently—at least if it had been a good hanging and the hangman knew what he was doing and the trap sprung right.

Kendricks had probably seen a hundred hangings in his thirty years, and still the most memorable had been that of a young stagecoach robber who'd had the misfortune of sticking up a powerful and vindictive Territorial representative. The trap hadn't worked quite right, and when the

Chippewa fell, he jerked funny and jerked too hard and jerked too angular, and so be damned if his head wasn't pulled right from his neck. Decapitated was the word the newspaper fellows used afterwards.

Kendricks sat with a schooner in the back of a saloon populated mostly by old men given to talking about the old days and playing pinochle for pennies. Kendricks liked being around old people. They didn't start fights and they knew a lot of interesting tales and they were appreciative of your friendship. They did not desert you the way one's peers did, especially women your own age. A few springs earlier Kendricks had been going to marry a woman named Alicia Bowman, and hadn't she been proud of him and his muscles and how other young men were afraid of him. How he didn't have to get all sweaty and dirty and tired when he worked, but instead had a nice clean job working for the owners of the Timbers—a "dude job" as Kendricks himself liked to describe it. Then it all went and ended over a stupid incident that had taken place one night at a dance, when a show-off type wearing a fancy silk vest and a lot of pomade on his hair had come up and asked Alicia to be his next partner, and Kendricks hadn't been able to stop himself. He grabbed the man and pushed him through the door to the soft night where he proceeded, in less than two minutes, to break the man's nose, jaw, and arm. The latter he'd done by getting the man in a kind of hammer-lock and twisting too hard at just the right moment.

He could scarcely recall the details of the incident, even though he'd had no more than two beers that evening.

All he knew was that he'd somehow managed to turn Miss Alicia Bowman into a shrieking and hysterical ex-fiancée, whom at least half a dozen people spent the rest of the night trying to calm down.

A few weeks later, after she refused all his calls at her door, he wrote her a letter and said he was sorry, but that he guessed his bad temper had been "brought over on the boat from Galway along with my Grandpa. But most men have tempers, so I hope you can forgive me being a little too frisky the other night."

He never heard from her again.

So now he sat here with the Territorial paper spread before him, looking for any stories about hangings, sipping from his schooner, occasionally looking up to watch fondly as one of the elderly gents won a hand at pinochle and exclaimed on it.

He was just lighting himself a cigar when he saw a shadow fall across his table, and there stood the man he'd been wondering about.

"You musn't be a very trusting soul," Frank Cord said.

"How's that, Mr. Cord?" Kendricks replied. His voice was always polite. His people were barely a generation off the boat and the prairie. Kendricks had no right to back talk a man like Mr. Cord here, and he would never think of it. He would have no trouble killing Mr. Cord, if that was required. But back talk him—no.

"I had assumed that you would go back to the Timbers for the next forty-eight hours. Instead you're staying right here in Danton."

"That's what Mr. Winters asked me to do. Those are just my orders."

Cord nodded to the schooner. "You mind if I sit down and talk a few minutes?"

Kendricks looked around behind him, as if somebody who mattered was sitting back there, and Kendricks just hadn't happened to notice him yet. "You want to sit down and talk to me?"

"If you don't mind."

"Well, hell's sake, I'd be honored." Kendricks would tell people at the Timbers about this moment. He would not tell the very important people such as Winters, but he would share the incident with the people of his own level. They would be suitably impressed that a man like Mr. Frank Cord had sat down and had a social talk with Kendricks.

Cord said, "How about bringing my friend and me two schooners?"

The bartender also looked suitably impressed. The Cords ran this town, and a Cord had never once put foot in this place before tonight.

The schooners came and Cord said, "I remember Mr. Winters talking about you."

"He's a very generous man. For Christmas last year he gave my pa a pocketwatch and my ma a gold fountain pen."

"He is a very generous man." Then Cord said, "Aren't you curious what he said about you?"

Kendricks shrugged. "Oh, I'm sure he said good things. He's an honest man. He's only been mad at me once, and he told me about it straight out. He's not like some people. If he's mad at you, he tells you to your face."

Cord leaned forward. "He told me there's practically nothing you're afraid of."

Kendricks laughed. "Oh, that isn't true, Mr. Cord. That's very nice of him to say, but it isn't true. I really am a-scared of mean dogs and every kind of snake there is."

Cord smiled. "But not of men."

Kendricks shrugged again. "No, I guess I'm not a-scared of any men I can think of."

"Good," Frank Cord said. "Good. Because then there's something I'd like you to help me with."

Kendricks, careful to be polite, said, "Mr. Cord, you'll remember now that I work for Mr. Winters."

"It's for Mr. Winters I'm proposing this."

"It is?"

"Yes." Cord sipped some beer. "What I'm going to

propose will ensure that Mr. Winters will have all his money within forty-eight hours and it will ensure one other thing.''

''What would that be, Mr. Cord?''

''It will mean that you come into five hundred dollars in greenbacks for yourself.''

''Five hundred dollars?''

''You mentioned your ma and pa.''

''Yes, yes, I did mention them.''

''Well, imagine the kind of presents you could buy them with five hundred dollars.''

Kendricks sat there and stared at the man. There were some men, men with sharp, mean laughs back at the Timbers, gamblers mostly, who said things about Kendricks every time he passed by.

Whispered about him.

Smirked about him.

So Kendricks sat there and stared at Frank Cord and wondered if he was that sort of man.

Kendricks said, ''I wouldn't want to get in any trouble with Mr. Winters.''

''Trouble?'' Cord said. ''Trouble? He'll thank you for helping me.''

But the longer Kendricks watched Cord, the more he had doubts about him. If you looked closely, you could see how Cord's fingers twitched, how his face was slick with sweat even though the temperature was mild, and how there was a certain crazed aspect in his eyes.

''I'm not sure about this, Mr. Cord.''

At which point Cord did something Kendricks had never seen done before.

Cord took from the inside pocket of his suit jacket a sleek leather wallet from which he carefully took five one-hundred-dollar bills.

He spread them out before Kendricks and said, ''This is your money you're looking at.''

"Oh, Mr. Cord," Kendricks said.

But he could not stop his heart from beating so quickly.

Or his mind from conjuring all the things he could do with such money.

Or his fingers from reaching out and touching the money.

Cord said, "It feels good, doesn't it?"

"I'd have to say yes, Mr. Cord, I'd have to say it feels good."

"Well, it should because it's all yours."

"It's a lot of money."

"But money you'll earn."

"And it won't make Mr. Winters angry?"

"On the contrary, it will make Mr. Winters very happy." He paused. "There's only one thing you have to promise me."

"What's that?"

"That you won't tell Mr. Winters—or anybody else— about this in advance. Not until the forty-eight hours are up."

Kendricks couldn't keep his eyes off the money.

Or his fingers, either.

"I guess I could promise that," Kendricks said.

"I'd have to have your absolute word."

"I guess I could give you that."

"You'd have to sound more positive than that," Cord said, pushing the money closer to Kendricks. "You'd have to sound a lot more positive."

Kendricks cleared his throat and said, "I could give you my absolute word."

"Would you do that? Would you give me your absolute word? Because if you'll do that, you can pick this money up right now and put it in your pocket, and it's all yours."

"If I just give you my absolute word?"

"That's all I need. Just that one thing. Your absolute word."

So Kendricks, who could no longer help himself the least little bit, scooped up the money—how green and crisp and good it felt—and put it in his shirt pocket and said, "Then you've got it, Mr. Cord. You've got my absolute word."

And didn't they smile. And didn't they shake hands, formal as politicians at some civic event.

Cord laughed. "That was some negotiation. How about another schooner and then we'll talk some?"

Kendricks couldn't imagine how envious the other workers at the Timbers would be if they ever learned that he'd had made five hundred dollars for doing a single job.

"That sounds like a fine idea," Kendricks said, unable to keep the smile from his face. "That sounds like a fine idea."

When Guild and Annie got back to the *Chronicle* office, they found the press humming away and Ruby and Maloney busy getting a paper out.

Maloney wore an inky apron and inky cotton protective sleeves and a four-cornered hat made from newspaper. He looked like a fat Irish kid inexplicably turned sixty years old by some mean witch.

"Meet my new apprentice," Ruby said, nodding to Maloney.

Guild said, "He tell you anything yet?"

Ruby said, "You would have been a big help to those folks who ran the Inquisition, Guild, you know that?"

Maloney smiled. "She's workin' on me, Guild. In her own way." He was stacking sheets of paper next to the hand-fed press. "I'd say her methods are likely to produce better results than yours."

Guild shook his head. "You sure know how to work people, don't you, Maloney? Remember how you got me

111

to buy you that bucket of beer before I took you into jail?''

Maloney laughed. "Not my fault I'm a likable sort."

Ruby glanced at Annie, who sat slumped in a straight-back chair. "She looks exhausted."

Guild nodded. "All the things that have been happening, it's no wonder." He told Ruby about their encounter with Karney and then what Mrs. Robertson had told them.

"Sounds strange," Ruby said. She was about to say more when Guild saw Annie, who had suddenly fallen asleep, sink from the chair to the floor.

He stalked across the room and picked her up. "Can she sleep in the same bed tonight?"

"Of course," Ruby said.

"I'll take her up."

"Give her a shot of bourbon to make sure she stays asleep for a long time. You'll find a bottle in my bedroom."

Maloney said to Ruby, "You wouldn't happen to have any of that bourbon down here, would you?"

Ruby said, "You just keep working there, Maloney. You're not *that* likable."

An hour earlier, a growing unease making either sleep or relaxation impossible, Mason Cord went to the bank run by his son. He still had a key—as well he should. It was still his bank, the last of the fortune he had made in the Territory before the McKenzie machine had put together Eastern money and begun to crush all other opponents.

Mason Cord's most trusted servant was a negro named Woodson. He was ebony of skin, white and kinky of hair, deferential of manner. Deferential, anyway, except for a few things, such as putting up with Mason Cord's temper, which he considered beneath him. "There ain't no more slavery, Mr. Cord," Woodson would say whenever Cord

112

exploded, reminding his wealthy employer of the war that had been fought two decades earlier—two million men being ground up in senseless rage—to settle just that issue. Among others. Then he would simply walk out of the room. He was at least ten years older than Mason Cord, and Mason Cord envied the hell out of Woodson's ease of movement and stamina. The old black bastard was made of steel.

It was Woodson who had brought Mason Cord to the bank tonight—in the fanciest surrey in this part of the Territory, everything but golden gilt trimming its sides— Woodson who sat guarding the doorway in his black frock coat and enigmatic brown gaze, a 12-gauge across his lap.

At first Cord just walked around in the bank. He took pride in his possessions. He noted the new carpeting, how the mahogany desks smelled sweetly of furniture polish, how orderly and tidy the teller cages looked. He thought of himself as a young man, the man who had built all this out of timber and rock and the blood of at least three different Indian tribes. McKenzie had taken everything else from him, by God, but he had not taken this bank.

Then his eyes fell on the bank vault. He would know soon enough what his son had been doing. Why Robertson had been murdered.

You killed accountants for one reason and one reason only.

Because they knew something you did not wish revealed.

Because they knew what was really going on with your operation.

Mason Cord, an old and tired man, a man who had built the largest fortune in the Territory only to see it diminished, a man who deserved a better son than the gods or biology had been willing to grant him—Mason Cord stood in front of the bank vault now and forced himself to take several deep breaths.

He approached the vault and then, almost as an after-thought, turned around and said to Woodson, "You have my permission to shoot anybody who tries to come through that door."

"But what if it's your son?"

"I said 'anybody,' didn't I?"

"Yes, sir."

"Then that's what I meant."

Mason Cord set to work on the combination. Within a minute he stood inside the vault and began his examination.

Chapter Fifteen

"One night I was with six men."

"Oh."

"Then another time I was with two men at once."

He didn't say anything. What could he say? He thought of how good it had felt to hold her, kiss her, to feel things he'd assumed were long dead in himself. Then he began hearing about her life, and he felt a terrible sorrow for her, for how things could get for young girls without folks out here in the Territory, and then he felt rage for how she'd been abused, and then, finally, he didn't know what to feel at all. He just went dead inside and listened.

"Then one time I worked in a house where they had girls as young as eight."

You could see the way moonlight gave the elm leaves shadow-life on the wall.

Guild and Annie had been upstairs now for an hour. He'd set her down in bed, thinking she would go right to sleep, but she hadn't.

So he'd gone and found the bourbon in the next room and brought it back. They both had some, a lot actually, and he rolled them both cigarettes, then Annie sort of scooched up against the wall and started crying very, very softly about Earle and everything that had happened to them over the last seven years.

"Then one night this man pulled a knife and cut me across the back. I was real scared."

Neither of them said anything for a time, and then Annie said, "I don't know what would have happened to me if Earle hadn't come along."

He looked over at her and nodded. The room smelled of sleep and bourbon and tobacco and violets outside the window.

"You'd better get to sleep," he said.

"I know you think he was nothing more than a cardsharp."

"It surprised me is all. At the inquest."

"He never cheated anybody who couldn't afford it."

Guild laughed, and turned to her. It was just like Annie to justify cardsharping in such a way. In the shadows she looked more beautiful and fragile than ever. He thought of their kiss again and then willed it from his mind. He took her hand. "I know you loved him, Annie, and I know everything he did for you. But we've all got to face up to what you've done."

"Well, there's nothing wrong with cheating a person like Frank Cord."

"Sure there is."

"He can afford it."

"That isn't the point."

She said, "You don't have no room to talk." She was angry.

"What's that supposed to mean?"

She started to say something and then stopped and then started again. "What Ruby told me."

"About what?"

"About you."

"What about me?"

"About the girl."

"The little girl?"

"Yes. The little girl."

So there it was, and that was just the way Annie would say it, of course. Right out front. The way a child would.

She said, "I shouldn't have said anything, Guild. I'm sorry. I swear on my locket I am. Ruby told me, and actually I felt sorry for you. She said it was your great sorrow and that it wasn't your fault."

"Maybe," Guild said, sighing.

He watched the shadows play on the wall. For a few moments he had felt close to Annie, thinking of the kiss and all, but now he was isolated again. You have to face what you've done, he'd just told Annie. And so he did.

She put her head on his shoulder. "I'm sorry, Guild. I just got mad is all. Ruby said it wasn't your fault. She truly did."

Guild shrugged. "Maybe it wasn't. I can't be sure."

"What happened?"

"I don't know if it's worth talking about."

"I thought we were partners."

"We are."

"Then you owe it to me, Guild. To talk." She paused. "I said I was sorry."

He sighed again. "It happened when I was a sheriff."

Given her distrust of the law—you couldn't come to your majority being a whore and have much respect for most lawmen, crooked as they were—her reaction was predictable. "God, she didn't tell me that. Did you have to wear a badge and everything?" She made it sound as if he'd worked in a leper colony.

He smiled. "Yes. A badge and everything."

"Well, I guess none of us is perfect, Guild. I mean, at least you ain't a lawman now."

117

He closed his eyes and thought back. To stalking a man named Bryce who'd pulled six stage robberies and managed to kill one person each time. He was a crazed man, bereft of a daughter who'd been mauled by a bear, and apparently driven crazy by his loss, one of those men who'd come to understand that existence had no meaning whatsoever and tried to impose a meaning on it by committing terrible acts.

He'd been stalking Bryce over near the sand hills. He was told by a blacksmith who'd just fixed a shoe for Bryce that the man was staying in a cabin near a northern leg of a nearby creek.

"So I rode up there and found the cabin, and I called out Bryce's name. I started up to the cabin with my rifle and then I saw something move just inside the door—something glint, like steel—and I knew it was a shotgun and so I fired and . . ."

For a time, neither said anything.

"The little girl had a shotgun?"

"Yes."

"Why was she alone?"

"Her folks were out in the field planting. There'd been some trouble with a sneak thief in those parts so they left a shotgun with her." He was back in it now. "I saw her face. She came out through the door, and she dropped the shotgun and just stood there, and I could see where I shot her in the chest. She just stood there staring at me, just staring at me, as if she didn't know what to do, whether to scream or fall down or cry. She just stood there, this little six-year-old girl in a gingham dress and brown hair and a pretty little face, and then she just fell down, and I couldn't even go near her for a while. I should have, should have run over to see if she was really dead, but I couldn't, I couldn't move. Then her folks came back and her mother was screaming and her father was hitting me in the face, but I didn't do anything, I just stood there the way the little girl had stood there, and I let him keep hitting me. I couldn't feel it anyway, I couldn't feel anything, all I could do was stand there. Just stand there.''

"Oh, shit, Guild," Annie said. "Shit."

She could obviously hear the hard and helpless remorse in his voice, and she drew him to her and then gently down to the bed, and this time when she kissed him it was so gently that it convulsed him, literally made him tremble.

And then abruptly the kiss changed and she took his face in her hands, and parted her lips and pressed herself even closer to him. "I've got the curse," she said. "I hope you don't mind."

"No," he said, "I don't mind at all." And he didn't, he didn't in the least.

The leaf patterns played on the wall and Guild found himself sinking into a wonderful darkness.

Woodson had been sitting at the door for an hour now.

The 12-gauge was getting heavy and he was getting tired.

He wondered what Mason Cord was doing in there. At first there had been a great deal of swearing, and then there had been the sound of boxes being overturned, as if in rage.

Since then there had been nothing.

So Woodson sat and waited.

Down the street you could hear the saloons, and further out you could hear dogs, and even further out you could hear trains.

Woodson was being lulled into a state of sleep by all these familiar noises when the gunshot came.

It seemed to explode and keep exploding within the confines of the huge vault.

"Lord," he said. "Lord."

He knew what he would find.

Knew exactly what he would find.

But he rushed to the vault anyway, and there on the floor was the old man.

Or what was left of the old man.

A .44 can take half a man's head if it's put just right on his teeth and its bullet allowed to travel up and out the back of his skull.

"Lord," Woodson said, leaning against the vault doorway. "Lord."

Then he ran on his old legs all the way out of the bank and all the way down the boardwalk past drunken idlers who had only scowls for negroes and finally, finally he reached the sheriff's office and found Sheriff Baines cleaning out his desk.

Chapter Sixteen

Guild heard a knock on the door at the bottom of the deep stairwell.

He looked over at Annie sleeping next to him. It had been long years since he'd felt the things her frightened little body had given him. He had clung to her there in the night. Clung.

Now he slipped from bed and pulled his pants on fast enough that they hurt his crotch. Then he grabbed his shirt and went down the stairs barefoot.

Past the curtained doorway, he saw a familiar silhouette. Baines.

"You all right?" Guild said.

"I guess."

"You look like shit."

"Thanks." Baines paused. "It's all coming undone."

"What's coming undone?"

"Seems like every goddamn thing."

"You want to come up?"

"It's all right?"

"It isn't likely Annie will shoot you."

Baines said, "Maybe she'd be doing me a favor."

"You're mighty good company tonight, Baines."

So they went up the stairs. Annie was asleep. They passed her room and went to a small alcove where there were two chairs. In the alcove were hung tintypes of three American presidents and Sitting Bull. Guild said, "Ruby just wants to cover her bets."

Baines hoisted his glass. "I guess I should celebrate."

"Celebrate what?"

"For a law type, you don't notice things worth a damn."

Guild looked at him. "You lost twenty pounds earlier tonight?"

"Look on my lapel, you stupid bastard." Baines wore a fancy leather suit jacket.

"Hell," Guild said after staring at the lapel a long time.

"Right there." Baines pointed to a certain spot on his coat. "Right there's where I used to wear my badge."

"What happened?"

Baines shrugged, then he told Guild about Mason Cord killing himself.

"What the hell's going on, anyway?" Guild asked.

"Only thing I can figure out is Frank Cord's in some kind of trouble."

Guild took some whiskey. "Robertson's widow said something to that effect, too. Said her husband had been acting very odd lately and that she'd seen him and Frank Cord arguing out in front of the Robertson place last week."

"She know what they were arguing about?"

"No. But she told me something else, too." Guild leaned forward. " She said that her husband had originally been hired by Mason Cord as not only an accountant, but as a kind of spy. Old Cord wanted Robertson to make sure that young Cord didn't make the same mess of the bank he'd made out of all his other businesses."

122

Baines said, "Leave it to Frank to figure out a way to buy somebody off."

"Robertson was a balding little runt. Easy enough to flatter him with money and a few girls."

Baines took a cigar from his pocket, bit off the end, put it in his mouth. He took out a lucifer, struck it against the doorframe. "You know what's going on here, Guild?"

"Not yet."

"You going to tell me if you figure it out?"

Guild said, "Now that you're not wearing a badge, I guess it'd be all right."

"He'll probably try to kill us both. Frank Cord, I mean."

"You scared?"

"A little."

Guild said, "That's about how much I'm scared, too."

They had some more whiskey and kept turning over speculations as to what might really be going on with Frank Cord.

Downstairs, Ruby and Maloney finished printing the newspaper. Ruby got some strawberry wine from a shelf, and they both had a glass and toasted each other. Ruby said, holding a *Chronicle* up to see, "Eugene would have been proud of me."

There was no mistaking the tears in her voice.

"Yes, he would have," Maloney said softly. He was tired but happy. He had not worked so hard in a long time. Not only had the labor been fulfilling, so had the time with Ruby.

"He was a fine man."

"I'll bet he was," Maloney said.

She laughed. "You look as if I said that as a slight." She leaned in and hugged him. "Come on now, Maloney. Just because I speak fondly of Eugene doesn't mean that I don't speak fondly of you. There's room enough in the world for at least two fine men, isn't there?"

"I guess." He sounded like an embarrassed teenager.

"At least there would be if one of those men told the truth about what happened at the jail the other night."

So there it was.

All these hours of eating, working on the paper, joking back and forth—she'd never said a word about it.

But now that had changed.

"It is time, you know, Maloney."

"I know."

"You think they'll kill you, don't you?"

"You know what they're like."

"Guild's here. He'll help you."

He stared out the front window. Just below the shade you could see the curve of the quarter-moon.

"I'm scared, Ruby."

"It'll be all right, Maloney. It really will."

"I'm the only one who really knows what happened the other night."

"Is that why they let you go free?"

He nodded. "They said if I didn't tell, they'd let me leave Danton whenever I wanted to. But that if I did tell, they'd make sure I was in Territorial prison within a week." He shrugged. He looked sad and helpless. "I don't know what to do, Ruby."

"You'll feel better if you tell the truth."

He said quickly, half-afraid to say it, "Being here to-night with you . . ."

She reached out her hand and held it there until he put his within it, and then she said, "It was the same for me, Maloney. You're a damn unlikely suitor, I have to say, but I like you."

But then his burden was on him again. "If I tell you,

they'll kill me. And if I don't tell, Guild will see to it that I go to prison."

Ruby said, "If you help bring Cord down, you might get clemency."

"You think so?" Maloney was looking for any kind of hope at all, and Ruby had just given it to him. "You think so, Ruby?"

"It's a possibility."

"You're not just saying that?"

"You're my friend, Maloney. I wouldn't lie."

"Would you go with me to the judge? Give me a character reference?"

She laughed. "I'm not sure how influential my word would be, but I'd sure go with you, Maloney. I sure would."

This part of the conversation seemed to give him back some of the high spirits he'd felt during dinner.

"Wonder what Baines wanted?" Maloney said, thinking about the fact that the sheriff had come here fifteen minutes ago looking for Guild. But they hadn't heard from him since.

"Maybe we'd better go find out." She took his arm. "Then you're going to sit down and tell me what really happened in that jail the other night, aren't you?"

And he looked at her and tried hard not to say the words that might doom him. But he said them anyway. "Yes, Ruby, then I'm going to sit down and tell you what really happened in that jail the other night."

"Good," Ruby said. "Now let's go find Guild and give him the good news."

So they went out the door, ready to climb the flight of stairs that would lead them to Guild, and that's when the rifle opened fire from across the street.

You could hear Maloney scream from three blocks away.

125

One bullet got him in the eye, the other in the heart.

Ruby threw herself over him, as if her body could smother the life escaping from him now, hold it within him.

"Maloney," she said. "Maloney."

Then from across the street, she heard footsteps running down the alley, toward the piney hills and the lonely coyotes.

Chapter Seventeen

The old man would never have permitted this. People who had no business wandering around his bank doing exactly that—and well beyond the area usually designated for the public.

Frank Cord sat in his office watching through the wide glass window, where he sometimes stood to watch the flow of customers. Except now he saw not customers but two of the odd-bird young male employees of Danton's oddest bird of all, Harcourt, the funeral home owner. They were carrying the old man out on a stretcher. He had been covered with a sheet but the blood and the brains had already soaked through, so that at its head the stretcher was a gummy, rusty-red color.

An hour ago, Woodson had come and got Frank and told him, and at first Frank's reaction had been simple—no. No, it was impossible. There were certain natural forces—the rising of the sun, tornadoes, the birthing of calves, the venerable existence of oaks and elms—and the old man's immortality had been one of them.

Harcourt came to the door. He was a plump man with wispy brown hair combed forward Roman senator–style so that people wouldn't notice how bald he was getting. He had never married. He said, "Mr. Cord, I think we'd better speak."

"What is it?"

"It's how I fill out the forms for the Territory, sir."

"What about them?" Cord did not like Harcourt. He did not like his odd-bird assistants. He did not like being around any of them.

"I'm just thinking of your father's reputation."

Cord laughed, shocking Harcourt. "My father's reputation as a beloved figure in the Territory?"

"No, sir, your father's reputation as a leading businessman. People will wonder, sir, how things were going for him if he . . . well, took his own life."

"So he had an accident?"

"Yes, sir, quite an incredible and unfortunate accident."

Cord smiled again. "My father was walking around inside the vault and he stumbled and fell on his gun and it discharged."

"Exactly, sir."

Cord's hands made fists, and his voice became a shout, and he came up from behind his desk. "He committed suicide. He put a gun in his mouth and pulled the trigger. That's what happened, and that's what you're to say, do you understand me?"

"Yes, sir. I understand."

"No, you don't. A man like you—what could you understand about my father?"

"Yes, sir."

"He built this goddamn town."

"Yes, sir."

"And it was his money that kept it prosperous."

"Yes, sir."

"He beat the wilderness, and he beat the Indians, and

he held McKenzie at bay for nine years. So don't tell me you understand my father.''

"Yes, sir.''

"Not somebody like you.''

"All right, sir.''

Harcourt's head dropped, and then Cord realized that, unlikely as it was, tears stood in his own eyes and voice. He had not loved his father, never had. You could not love a man so hard or harsh, but now his father was gone, and Cord felt a curious loneliness, as if the only certainty in his life had been taken away.

Harcourt said, "Is that all you'll be needing?''

Cord looked across at the much-gossiped-about man. Saw his words had stung the man and said, "I shouldn't have talked to you like that.''

"It's all right, sir.''

"No, it isn't all right, Harcourt. You don't have to take people's abuse. You let them abuse you too much.''

"Yes, sir.''

There was no hope. He said, "My father killed himself because he'd been in poor health.'' Harcourt was a gossip. He'd give him a logical story and let him disseminate it.

"Yes, sir.''

"He did not want to become what he called 'pathetic' in his final days. So he came down here and killed himself.''

"Yes, sir.''

"That's what to put on your report.''

"Yes, sir.''

"I want him to have at least the dignity of the truth.''

"Yes, sir.''

Cord sat back down at his desk. "Sorry I was so harsh, Harcourt.''

"Yes, sir.''

Yes, sir, Cord thought. The bastard was hopeless.

Harcourt nodded and was gone, leaving Cord to sit and stare at the stack of ledgers that had been sitting in the vault with the old man, the ledgers he'd brought in from Robertson's office.

The old man had figured it out, no doubt about that.

Figured out that he was ruined, and figured out that his son Frank had been the one responsible.

Figured out that he could not face a community over which he had reigned for three decades as charitable despot.

Cord sat back and put his hands over his face, pressed them very tight, so that there was complete blackness. He felt safe in the blackness. When, as a boy, he'd displeased his father, he used to go up in the attic of the mansion and hide there. In the western corner, under the eave, there was total and complete blackness—it was as if he were drifting in some kind of void, and he felt safe from the old man. But eventually would come the sound of footsteps up the stairs—the old man with his strop. The beatings had been vicious. Sometimes his mother had tried to intercede, and sometimes even Woodson had tried to intercede, but when the old man got to the point that he took his strop from its special place in his bottom bureau drawer, a madness befell him and . . .

Then Cord began to let his mind drift to the image of the South Sea Islands he kept with him like a religious relic. He could smell the breezes, feel the skin of an impossibly erotic native girl. . . .

Tomorrow afternoon the Wells Fargo stage would be here. The payroll. Enough to keep him comfortably for the rest of his life. By tomorrow night—

A knock roused him.

Kendricks stood in the doorway. The short, massive man was impossible to read. He said, without a hint of his feelings, "It's done, Mr. Cord."

"By God," Cord said, and he sounded so happy there was a hint of hysteria in his voice. "You really are good, aren't you?"

Typically, instead of boasting, Kendricks only looked embarrassed, as if he were being vastly overpraised. "It wasn't hard, Mr. Cord. It was just a shot across the street and there was a gas lamp nearby so I could see what I was doing real good and—well, it wasn't hard."

So that was the last of it.

Maloney was dead.

Cord knew that Maloney would tell what he knew about the other night in jail. If Judge Harnack were to find this out before Cord left town with the payroll . . .

So he'd had Karney let Maloney go free. It was easier to kill him outside of jail than inside, especially since Hammond had also been killed in jail.

Cord said, "So what do you do to celebrate?"

Kendricks just shrugged. "I like malts, Mr. Cord."

"Malted milks?"

Kendricks nodded. "Especially chocolate ones."

Cord roared. He found this wonderfully funny. By God, wasn't it funny? "You go out and kill a man and you could have liquor and women, and instead you want a chocolate malted?"

"I guess so, Mr. Cord." Kendricks was beginning to look confused, as if he didn't understand what Mr. Cord was making all the fuss about.

"Then, dammit, that's exactly what we're going to do, Kendricks."

"What's that, Mr. Cord?"

"We're going to go find you the best chocolate malted in the Territory." And he got up and went over to Kendricks and threw his arm around him and said, "How about that, Kendricks? Doesn't that sound good? The best chocolate malted in the Territory?"

131

Kendricks was giving him very strange looks. Very strange.

But all he said was "Yes, Mr. Cord, that does sound good. Real good."

Half an hour earlier, the doctor had come in and put his stethoscope here and put his stethoscope there and then picked up Maloney's hand and felt for a pulse in the wrist. He put his finger on Maloney's carotid artery, then turned to Ruby and said, "I'm afraid he's dead."

They were gathered in the downstairs office of the *Chronicle*—Guild, Annie, Ruby, Baines.

They had laid Maloney out on a table and put a pillow under his head and a quilt over his body.

He had died in spasms, the way sick cats and dogs died, jerking and twitching, eyes so glassy they resembled milky marbles.

He'd just twitched and jerked, and then he started to drool, and they could even see his feet start to jerk around, as if keeping time to some unheard fiddle tune. It was almost comic, the way his feet jumped around inside his old brown shoes with the holes in the soles and the leather worn through even on the uppers. He had tried to say some things, but it was far too late for that.

After the doctor put his stethoscope back in his bag, he said to Baines, "You going to try to stop it?"

"I'm not the Law any more."

"I guess you weren't a hell of a lot more help when you were the Law, Baines, being Frank Cord's toady and all."

"You done?" Guild said.

The doctor glared at him. "Yeah, I'm done, and if something doesn't happen soon, so's this town."

132

He picked up his bag and nodded his condolences to Ruby and left.

Guild could see that the doctor's words had shamed Baines. Guild said softly, "You all right, Baines?"

"I had it coming."

"Maybe half of it."

Annie went to Maloney's head and touched him. Her hand flicked away as if she'd been burned. "He's already cold." She said it with terrible awe.

"It's going to shit," Baines said, "all of it. And maybe now we've got a chance to get Cord."

"Maybe," Guild said.

"You two shut up," Ruby said. Then she nodded to Annie, who was saying a prayer over Maloney.

"Can't you goddamn bow your heads?" Ruby said.

They bowed their heads while Annie muttered words so quiet they couldn't be heard by anybody else.

Ruby's eyes got silver with tears.

Guild went over to her, slid his arm around her. "I'm glad you made me ease off him," he said, nodding to Maloney.

She laughed and cried at the same time. "Yeah, Guild, so am I." She snuffled tears. "He was going to tell everything he knew."

Guild nodded. His skepticism wasn't hard to see. Ruby exploded. "Don't stand there being so goddamn smug, Guild! He told me he was going to tell what he knew and I believed him! If anybody should have sympathy for somebody like Maloney, it should be you! You may not have meant to kill that little girl, but it made you an outcast anyway! Just the way Maloney was an outcast!"

"Ruby!" Annie said.

Ruby waved a helpless hand, sighed. "He knows I didn't mean anything by it. You know that, don't you, Guild? I'm sorry, Guild. I shouldn't have said that."

Shaking his head, Guild said, "I shouldn't have been so hard on him, Ruby. You're right." He spread his arms around her and she came inside and he hugged her.

Baines said, "Anybody else hungry?"

"I am, kind of," Annie said.

"I could use some coffee, anyway," Guild said.

"Maybe over breakfast," Baines said, "we can figure out what the hell's going on around here."

Chapter Eighteen

Even though it was scarcely dawn, the restaurant was crowded with day laborers getting ready for a ten-hour stint, for which they would be paid thirty cents an hour.

The air was blue with smoke and coarse with the rumble of hungover voices as the waiter, a Greek with an apron already soiled from slicing ham and bacon, led them to a large table in the back, beneath a painting of the Territorial flag. The Greek paid a lot of deference to Baines. He was obviously under the impression Baines was still sheriff.

"You get the special," the Greek said to Baines when they were all seated.

"What's that?" Baines asked.

"Three eggs for the price of two."

"I don't want eggs," Ruby said. "I want whiskey."

The Greek looked surprised. "Wasn't it your paper that ran the editorial on temperance, Ruby?"

"The hell with temperance," Ruby said. "I want some damn whiskey."

The Greek checked with Baines for permission. Baines said, "Breakfast for everybody except Ruby. You bring her some bourbon, all right?"

"You know it's against the ordinance, sheriff, me servin' liquor."

"You mean you don't have any whiskey on the premises?"

"I didn't say that."

"Good. Then bring it."

When the Greek left, Annie leaned into Ruby and hugged her and said, "I know what you're thinking, Ruby, but don't worry. We'll get our chance to kill him. I promise you.'

Baines said, "Guild, you're not really going to let her kill Cord, are you?"

Guild smiled. "Not unless she gets a clean shot at him."

Baines seemed offended. "Maybe I've been a lawman too long, but it's a hell of a fine day when ladies sit around restaurants drinking bourbon at barely five A.M. discussing coldblooded murder."

Breakfast came. Everybody started eating. Except Ruby. She started drinking. The Greek had brought her a bottle. She had had two belts before Guild got a single bite of egg in his stomach.

Guild said, "We know one thing for sure."

"What?" Annie said.

"Robertson was killed because he knew something Frank Cord couldn't afford to have revealed."

Baines said, "Something so bad that Mason Cord found out and killed himself over it."

Then the Greek was back. "How is everything?"

"Everything's fine," Ruby said, "except I'm out of whiskey."

Everybody looked at her and then at the pint bottle, and damned if she hadn't drained it.

"Coffee for her," Guild said.

"I don't take any damn orders from you, Guild—not after the way you treated Maloney."

"I'm sorry about how I treated Maloney, and I'm sorry that I'm going to force coffee down you, but I am. Otherwise I'll have to hit you right here in public."

She was drunk and took him seriously. "You're the kind of man who'd hit a woman?"

He grinned. "Not in public—unless it's absolutely necessary."

So the Greek went and got Ruby a big glass mug of steaming coffee. In the meantime they sat at the table speculating on all the things that had taken place in the past forty-eight hours.

Thinking aloud, Baines said, "What could Robertson have known about Frank Cord?"

Annie laughed. "That there wasn't any money in the bank."

Baines said, "Well, I wish it were that simple, Annie. But there is money in the bank. I drew out nearly five hundred yesterday to send to my oldest son back East."

Guild said, "But what if there isn't as much money as there should be?"

"Embezzlement?" Baines asked.

Guild nodded.

Baines set his coffee cup down hard. " Goddammit, Guild, you know that's about the only thing we could be dealing with here, isn't it? There isn't much else Robertson *could* have known about Cord."

Guild was about to talk when the Greek returned. Guild was getting real tired of the Greek's solicitude. Real tired. He was just weary enough to be grumpy and just grumpy enough to say something to the Greek. He started to speak up, but the Greek spoke first.

"Sheriff, there's something queer going on in the town square."

"What's that?" Baines asked.

"You better come see."

137

Baines looked at Guild. "You come with me?"

"Sure."

"You ladies excuse us?"

"Who said we're ladies?" Ruby snarled from the table.

She was so drunk she appeared to be permanently canted to the right.

"Watch her. Carefully. All right?" Guild said to Annie.

"You just remember your promise. Who gets to do the shooting."

"I remember."

Baines made a face and then led the way out of the restaurant. On the way out, he said, "You think she's all right?"

"Annie?"

"Yeah."

"How do you mean?"

"In the head."

"Sure. She just really wants to kill Cord."

All Baines said was "Oh."

Out on the boardwalk you could see the moisture from the night. The sky was blue-streaked and the sun was already a round, warm ball, and you could hear mudwagons clattering and a train at the depot pulling in.

By the time they reached the town square, several passersby had already given Baines and Guild curious glances.

They soon found out why.

In the middle of the square, between the oval bandstand and the Civil War memorial, stood a line of ragged men, ten in all, who were listening to Frank Cord and a squat, muscular man.

"What's going on?" Guild said.

Baines said, "Duck in that building front over there and wait for me."

138

"Why?"

"Because if Cord sees you, he'll arrest you on the spot."

Now it was Guild's turn to say "Oh."

Baines went on ahead to the square. As he walked, he watched a curious ceremony take place. From his pocket, Frank Cord had taken a brass star. He pinned it on one of the line of ragged men Baines recognized as unemployed cowhands and drifters. Then Cord went on to the next man, took out a second brass star, and pinned it on.

"You starting an army?" Baines asked when he reached Cord.

Cord and a man named Kendricks turned to face him.

Cord said, "Since you're no longer sheriff, I'd say it isn't any of your business."

"You're not actually deputizing these men, are you?"

"As I said, Baines, that's my business."

"Frank, for Christ sake, think of your father. He built this town. He wouldn't want these men wearing badges."

Kendricks said, "Do you need any help, Mr. Cord?"

"Not at the moment." Cord nodded to the men. "I've talked with the city council and we've decided we need twenty-four hours of martial law for the sake of stability."

Baines snorted. "This sure looks like a crack outfit."

The line of men glared at Baines. He glared back. "Half of them you've had me run in from time to time."

"People change," Cord said sardonically.

"Yeah, every one of these boys looks like he's had the calling, all right."

Kendricks came up to Cord and whispered something to him. Slowly, Kendricks angled his head so he could get a glimpse of something past the Civil War memorial, past the edge of the bandstand, past the row of park benches that ringed the square.

Kendricks whispered something else.

Then Baines noticed how the squat man began to ease away from Cord.

Baines sensed what was happening. Already moving, backing up some, he said, "I just hope you don't pull the whole town down with you, Frank."

The gunshot ripped into the elm just to the left of Cord's head.

Startled, Cord dove for the ground, as did several of the other men.

Baines took the opportunity he had been given. He moved fast—not quite running because of his size and because he smoked too damned much—to leave the park and get back to the street, where Guild was hiding in an alley. A crowd had already gathered, trying to figure out where the shot had come from.

"How'd you know to shoot?"

"Saw the short man starting across the grass to me."

"We'd better get the hell over to the restaurant." Baines looked behind him.

Cord and the men were gathering themselves. In moments they'd start running over here.

They reached the Greek's out of breath and slick with sweat. They pushed past other diners and reached the table.

Guild grabbed Annie, told her breathlessly what was happening. "Meet us in the bluffs, at Indian Point, near noon. Bring rifles."

Ruby, drunker than before, was trying to focus her eyes and see what was going on.

"You know where we can get horses?" Guild asked Baines.

"Not good ones. But they'll do."

"Fine," Guild said. He looked back at Annie now. Her eyes were damp from tears.

Guild smiled. "Come on now."

"I'm scared for you is all. Don't make a thing of it."

He reached out and she took his hand. It was a child's hand but soon it would be a woman's. He held it a long moment, and then he heard shouts from the front of the restaurant and knew that Cord's new deputies were there.

"Noon," Guild said.

Annie said, "I wish I'd told you everything in my heart last night." She touched her locket. "A person should do things like that, Guild. They really should."

Gunfire roared through the restaurant as one of the deputies opened fire with a shotgun.

Baines, crouching, said to Guild, "That's a real high caliber of lawman, wouldn't you say? Opening fire with a goddamn shotgun in a crowded restaurant."

Guild saw where they had to go to get to the kitchen and out the back door.

He glanced once more at Annie, wishing he'd said all that had been in his heart last night, too, and then he said to Baines, "You ready to get your ass shot off?"

"Not ready," Baines said, "but willing."

They ran for the kitchen and their only chance at escape.

Chapter Nineteen

They ran down a dusty alley past a clutch of small children, who yelled out at the sheriff in admiration and awe.

At a red barn, the sheriff turned in, taking out his weapon as he did so.

A blacksmith, working at the anvil, sweated out already for the day, looked up when he heard footsteps. When he saw the sheriff's drawn gun, his thick face developed a tic. "Everything all right, Sheriff?" He looked to be just as struck with authority as the tots had been.

"You got a couple of horses you can saddle up fast?"

"Reckon."

"How about doing it?"

"Sure." He shrugged wide shoulders and set to work.

Guild rolled a cigarette, paced.

When they heard harsh human noises at the opposite end of the alley a few minutes later, Guild glanced at Baines.

"You think you could hurry that up a little, Harold?"

Harold shrugged again. "Sure. Like I say, you're the sheriff."

Hearing footsteps running toward them, Guild drew his weapon, too.

Finally, Harold finished with the second bridle. "Ain't what you'd call prizes."

"That's fine. Appreciate it."

"Least I can do, you being the sheriff and all."

Guild and Baines swung up on their horses.

"Not any more I'm not," Baines said as they clattered out of the barn and headed for the road out of town.

They were scarcely around the first turn, then yards away, when three deputies ran into the bar, dropped to their knees, and opened fire with Remington repeaters.

A strange man greeted Annie and Ruby.

Or rather didn't greet them.

Annie and Ruby were led into the sheriff's office, where Kendricks sat eating pancakes brought over to him from the hotel down the street. He did not seem interested at all in the two women.

"You mind telling us why we're here?" Annie said.

Kendricks looked up. He had a face wide as a buffalo. His mouth was slick with syrup. "I don't rightly know, Miss."

Annie had expected a harsh remark. Instead, the small, wide man was polite. Very polite.

"You didn't call us here?"

"No, I didn't, ma'am."

"Then who did?"

"I guess it must have been Mr. Cord."

Kendricks quit eating long enough to glance up at the two deputies. "It was Mr. Cord who wanted to see them, wasn't it?"

The deputies nodded.

"That being the case, and Mr. Cord not being here, Miss, why don't you two sit down over there, if you'd like."

"Just who the hell are you?" Ruby demanded. Coffee and walking around had sobered her up reasonably well.

"My name is Mitchell Kendricks, ma'am." He smiled his syrupy smile. "I know who you are. You're the newspaper lady. My ma, she reads the *Chronicle* all the time. Really likes it."

But Ruby was in no mood for flattery. "You still haven't answered my question."

"I told you."

"You told me your name is all. What I mean is what are you doing wearing the sheriff's badge and sitting behind that desk?"

Kendricks touched the brass badge as if he'd just noticed it for the first time. "Oh. The badge. Well, Mr. Cord asked me to be temporary sheriff."

"That your pay?" Ruby said, nodding to his empty plate.

Kendricks looked confused.

"The way you're eating them, a soul would swear they were solid gold."

Kendricks laughed softly. His gentle manner was eerie in a man his size and demeanor. "No, ma'am, he'll pay me in greenbacks."

Kendricks had just finished talking when the door opened up and Cord himself came in.

Ruby said, "You don't look so good, Frank."

He glared at her. "First time I've ever known you to be concerned with my welfare."

"Somebody has to be, now that your pa can't fight your battles any more."

"You'd better take account of my mood, Ruby. You'd better take account real good."

Annie had to keep her head down. She could not stand to watch the man. She was afraid of what she would do.

Her hand moved to the handle of her Peacemaker.

"Why the hell did these two street urchins drag us over here, Frank?" Ruby said.

"I want to find out where Guild and Baines went. I figured you'd know."

"Don't know a thing."

"You're a damn liar, Ruby, and you know it."

"You're forgetting, Frank. You're the liar, not me. You lied to your pa, you lie to your wife, you lie to this whole town."

Kendricks said, "Excuse me, ma'am."

"What?" Ruby said.

"I don't like to speak out of turn, but I don't think you have no call to talk to Mr. Cord like that."

Cord laughed. "I wish she shared your respect for me, Kendricks." Then the smile vanished, and he looked old and no longer especially handsome, puffy really, from food and years and the long anguish of failure. "Ruby, for Christ's sake, you and I are old enemies, but we've kept it within bounds. Don't push too far today. Please."

And that was when Annie moved.

She tore the Peacemaker from between her butternuts and her white blouse, moving her hand beneath her coat so the deputies could not see until she had the weapon completely exposed.

Kendricks saw it first.

A betting man would have laid odds against the speed with which the bulky little man moved.

But before Annie could get off a clean shot at Cord, Kendricks had slammed into her and knocked her back into the wall, the gun discharging into the ceiling.

Immediately, Ruby jumped on Kendricks and began pulling him off Annie, who was already sobbing in frustration.

Cord came over and stood above them. "Your little slattern friend here just made a very bad mistake, Ruby."

145

"Tell him to get off her," Ruby said.

"It's all right, Kendricks. You can let her up."

Annie got up, brushing herself off, her face scarlet with anger. "I'm still goin' to kill you, Cord." She touched her locket. "And that's a promise."

Cord said, "Until she took a shot at me, Ruby, I didn't have any legal right to hold either one of you. Now I guess that's changed."

To his deputies, he said, "Take them back and put them in a cell."

"Yes, sir."

One of them reached for Annie. She slapped him with the force of a shot. "Don't touch me," she said.

Cord smiled. "I would think you'd be used to being touched by now, Annie."

"Not no more," she said, jerking herself even further away from the deputy. "Not since Earle got me away from that house and that madam." She went up to him and spat directly into his face. "And you killed Earle. You and nobody else."

Cord just stood there and stared at her a long moment, and then he slapped her with a fury that backed her up three feet.

Cord said to Ruby, "I told you, Ruby. I told you you'd better be careful of me."

Ruby, angry, just shook her head.

Kendricks came back over and stood dutifully alongside Cord.

Then Cord nodded to his deputies and they took the women away.

Chapter Twenty

Indian Point was a jagged chunk of red sedimentary rock half-concealed by a small forest of ponderosa pine and cedar trees and grass deep enough in places to cover your shoulders. The Point overlooked a stage road some two hundred feet below. To the east was a swing station for Wells Fargo. When the first white settlers came to the Territory, they often found themselves attacked from the Point. It was virtually impregnable.

At noon, Guild and Baines sat in a clearing near the Point, watching a doe which, in turn, watched a monarch butterfly perform various astonishing feats.

Baines hauled out his pocketwatch and said, "We said noon."

"They'll be here."

"What if they don't come? What if Cord is holding them?"

"You said the judge is honest."

Baines laughed. "I said he's honest if you can shame him into it. There's a difference. If Cord gave him a good reason to hold Annie and Ruby, the judge probably wouldn't say much at all."

"If he does have them, we're going to have a hell of a time getting them back."

Baines nodded. "Cord has probably got twenty men deputized now."

Guild shook his head, spat, got up. Waiting always made him restless. He walked out to the edge of the Point, looked down on the stage station. There was a rope corral out back. A few horses with nose bags stood inside. He had some of his cigarette and enjoyed for a moment the smells of sunshine and nearby mint, and then he said, "Damn."

"What?"

"Come here."

"Christ, Guild, I'm pretty tired. Couldn't you just sort of tell me from there?"

"Get over here, Baines."

Baines sighed and struggled to his feet and went over to Guild. "Look."

Baines looked. "Beautiful this time of year, isn't it?"

"The swing station down there and the Wells Fargo stage."

"What about it?"

Guild inhaled his cigarette deeply enough that the tobacco taste was almost sweet. "Remember back at the restaurant this morning, talking about Cord?"

"I guess."

"We said maybe he was embezzling or something."

"Right." Baines still sounded tentative, confused.

"You know much about the bank's operations?"

"Some, I guess."

"Do they get large shipments of greenbacks from any place on a regular basis?"

"Sure," Baines said. "From up near the border. There are still some gold-mining operations left from the boom days and there are grain trusts, too. Once a month it comes. By stage. And they put considerable money in the bank. We used to have to double up on deputies sometimes.'' Then he said, ''Damn.''

''What?''

''It should be about the right time of month.''

Guild had some more of his cigarette, walked out further to the edge of the Point to look down. For a moment he lifted his head. He felt as part of the vast, blue prairie sky. A chicken hawk rode the air currents.

Baines said, ''You thinking?''

''I'm trying.''

''What are you thinking about?''

''How about shutting up a minute?''

''All right. I need to go over to that big ponderosa, anyway, and empty my bladder.''

''I'm happy for you.''

Baines went over and relieved himself, and when he came back Guild said, ''That's how he's doing it.'' He nodded down to the swing station.

''Doing what?''

''Embezzling.''

''How?''

''He embezzles what he needs—for gambling mostly, I assume, from what Mrs. Robertson said—and he just goes from month to month. When the Wells Fargo folks come every month, he's all right for a while.''

''Wouldn't his father have found out? He hired Robertson to watch over his son.''

''He paid Robertson off. Girls. Liquor. Flattery. Robertson fixed the books for him.''

''Damn.''

''And that's what Earle Hammond must have overheard when he was at the bank that night. Robertson and Cord talking. Cord couldn't afford to let Earle live—even though Earle was so drunk he wouldn't have remembered a damn

149

thing. Then Cord must have seen that he could get rid of both Earle and Robertson and blame Earle for it."

"Why would he kill Robertson?"

"Simple enough. Somebody knows that much about you, they become a burden."

Baines sighed. "I'm an old bastard, Guild. My people are all dead. I want to be sitting on some hotel veranda out in California listening to the ocean and having plump young whores tease me. How the hell did I ever get into this?"

"You got lazy and you got scared and you got greedy."

"I sound like one hell of an admirable man."

Guild's jaw muscles worked and he said, "Well, at least you haven't killed a six-year-old girl."

There was an edgy silence, then Baines said, "You got to ease up on yourself, Guild. You know that?"

"I expect I do."

They listened to the jays and wrens for a time, and then Guild took out his watch and said, "I'm starting to agree with you."

"What?"

"Annie and Ruby aren't coming."

"What're we going to do?"

Guild turned and faced him. There was a grin on his face, and despite his gray hair and the age lines around his eyes, he looked almost boyish. "Well," he said, "the first thing we're going to do is buy ourselves some stage tickets, and then we're going to ride into Dalton."

"With Cord's deputies everywhere?"

"They won't be able to see us inside the stage until it's too late."

"You sure?"

Guild laughed. "I'm not going to put it in writing, if that's what you mean."

Baines said, "I figured as much."

All Guild said was, "You got a few greenbacks for the stage tickets?"

The judge bit off tobacco from a tangy cut he held in his rough hand and said, "Just what the hell's going on here anyway, Frank?"

"Things need to calm down. I'm just trying to help them along."

They were in the courthouse. The judge had summoned Frank here. "People are damned stirred up." He got up, walked to the window, looked down on the street. "They don't know what's going to happen next and they don't like the idea of armed men patrolling the streets." He turned back from the window, brushed some dandruff from the shoulder of his black robe. "And I hear you've arrested Ruby Gillespie and that cute little prostitute."

"I've got three witnesses to the fact that they took a shot at me. The girl did, anyway."

The judge just looked at him. "Now why would she go and do a thing like that?"

Cord, sensing irony in the judge's voice, said, "I don't know."

"It couldn't be that you and Karney weren't telling the truth about who killed Robertson and what really happened in the jail the other night, could it?"

"What we said at the inquest was the truth."

The judge shook his head. "And you said Baines is with the man Guild?"

"Yes."

"And where are they?"

"We're looking for them."

The judge went over and sat back down and said, "I did a lot of favors for your father."

"I appreciate that."

The judge spat into a fancy brass spitoon. He sat back, surrounded by a huge Stars and Stripes hung behind him. "I believed, or convinced myself that I believed, that even if your father was not quite an honest man, that the things he did were a benefit to the Territory. So I went along with him unless he asked me to do something I just couldn't face. Your cousin, for instance, once raped a pregnant Indian woman. As you know, he's still in Territorial prison, despite all your father's pleas."

"Nobody ever asked you to be a whore."

The judge laughed. "Well, not exactly, anyway."

Cord was getting impatient. He was being chastised in some oblique way. He had many things to do.

"But now," the judge said, "your father's dead, and things are different."

"Meaning?"

"Meaning that I won't make the same allowances for you that I did for him." The judge raised his gavel and looked at it as if examining it for flaws of some sort. "It's time I be a judge again." He raised his eyes to Cord's. "I want a city council meeting tonight, and I want a new sheriff tomorrow—a real one—and I want all these pieces of trash you've deputized to go back to the gutter."

"All right."

"And one more thing."

"Yes?"

"I don't want any of those damn punks you hung stars on to hurt anybody. Not anybody at all, for any reason at all."

"I'll see to it."

Cord nodded and was turning to leave when the judge spoke again. He said, "You're not strong, the way your father was. And it would be a serious mistake if you tried to be."

Cord glared at him and left.

When Cord's footsteps were heard deep on the ground floor then going out the front door, the judge angled his head to the cloakroom and said, "Hanratty, get in here."

A big man in a yellow corduroy suit and a black derby came in. "Follow Frank Cord the rest of the day. I want to know everything he does. Get back to me around supper-time."

Hanratty smiled. "I never liked that bastard, anyway."

The judge smiled back. "You're a clerk of this court, Hanratty. You're supposed to keep a civil tongue and an open mind."

"Right, Your Honor," Hanratty said. "Right."

He left, taking the stairs two at a time, and then he caught up with Frank Cord and fell into following him at a judicious distance.

Chapter Twenty-One

"I miss him, Ruby. Damn but I do."

Several times Ruby had asked Annie to quit walking off the small clear space inside their cell. But the frail blonde girl was too charged to stop pacing and fidgeting.

"He did you some real favors," Ruby said.

"He surely did," Annie said. "He surely did."

Ruby, sober now, sat on the edge of one of the straw-tick cots. She felt old and weary beyond her years, as if every moment of hardship here in the Territory had taken a sudden overwhelming toll.

"I wish I'd told him everything—well, everything I felt."

Ruby had never seen Annie blush before.

Ruby put out her rough hands and Annie came over and took them.

"Oh, Ruby, I hope he's all right."

Ruby wondered if she was as sober as she'd thought. "Of course, he's all right, honey. His body's in the ground and his soul . . ." Ruby raised her eyes. "And even though he wasn't exactly what you'd call an angel, I'm sure his soul is up there."

"His soul? What are you talking about, Ruby?"

"Earle—"

"Earle! Not Earle, Guild!"

So then it all made sense. Ruby sat there and rubbed her face and touched her hand to her aching head. Between coffee and a ragged nap, she felt as if she'd been slapped into a terrible kind of sobriety. Ruby said, "Guild understands how you feel about him."

"How do you know?"

"Because when he talks about you, his voice gets softer. That's always a sure sign with men. When their voices get softer."

Annie clung to Ruby's hands. "I hope you're right, Ruby. I hope that's what it means when a man's voice gets soft."

"Why don't you come over here and sit down next to me, honey? You're making me crazy walking around all the time."

"All right, Ruby."

So they sat next to each other on the straw tick and looked around at the dungeonlike cells and the maze of iron bars and smelled the urine and stale food and loneliness.

"You know, Ruby, there's only two things I want in the world." She paused. "I want to kill Frank Cord and I want to put on my fancy white dress and go to a nice clean restaurant with Guild." Her blue, blue eyes surveyed the place. "Being here reminds me of Earle. . . ." Then, after a pause, she said, "We were supposed to meet them at Indian Point. Now we ain't going to."

"Aren't going to."

Annie laughed softly. "You and Earle."

Ruby sighed suddenly and said, "I can't take this anymore."

"What?" Annie said, sounding afraid that she'd offended Ruby in some way.

"I've got to see some damn sunlight."

Annie jumped up. She got a small footstool and placed it over by the small barred window that opened on a side street.

Ruby said, "Thank you, honey."

Then she went over and stood on the stool and looked up at the sky and the rolling white clouds. She could smell apple blossoms. She closed her eyes, inhaled, as if taking in deeply some exotic perfume.

Then a hard little voice said, "Just what the Sam hill are you doing in there, Ruby Gillespie?"

Ruby opened her eyes. Down on the street, staring up at her, was Mrs. Palmer, Danton's leading crank. She had a lot of money in the bank, and since the death of her husband, it was all she worried about. As usual, she carried a parasol too girly for her years and the unremitting gaze of a contented hangman.

"Frank Cord put me here," Ruby said. Much as anybody could be friends with Mrs. Palmer, Ruby was. Mrs. Palmer had been won over when Ruby did an editorial on why women should be given the right to vote.

"Frank Cord? Why would he do that?"

"Who you talking to?" Annie asked.

Ruby turned around. "To a friend of mine. Just be patient, honey."

Annie frowned as if she'd been deserted.

Ruby went back to Mrs. Palmer. "Where are you going?"

"Have to get some things at the market. But I better stop by the bank first for a withdrawal." She shook her head. "Believe me, Ruby, I'm going to have a talk with Frank Cord about just what you're doing in jail." Then she made a little fist. "Damnation, I'm going to talk to other people, too."

"I'd appreciate it if you would, I certainly would."

"Can I bring you anything? Would you like a piece of poundcake from the bakery or something?"

"No, I'm fine. Fine."

Then Mrs. Palmer fell to shaking her head again. "Terrible thing about Mason Cord, wasn't it? His health, I'm told."

"I don't think that was it."

Mrs. Palmer said, "What?" as if she'd been told the most scandalous secret she'd ever heard.

"I think it was because his whole empire was crumbling."

"But not the bank. The bank is all right, isn't it?"

Then an awful thought came to Ruby—awful because of her friend Mrs. Palmer here. She hesitated just a second about using Mrs. Palmer in such a devious way and then decided she had no choice.

"You remember how the bank collapse was in sixty-three?" Ruby said.

"I don't even like to think about it."

Ruby nodded in the general direction of the bank. "I think it could be happening again."

"Are you serious?"

"Very serious."

"But Good Lord, my money—"

"Everybody's money."

"But I was in the vault just the other day. There was plenty—"

Ruby said, remembering the conversation Guild and Baines had had at the restaurant, "There's always some money, but is there enough money?"

"Good Lord." Mrs. Palmer looked forlorn. "Do you think there's still time to get my money?"

"If you move quickly enough."

"Take it all out?"

"That's what I'd do."

"Good Lord."

"You'd better hurry."

"Yes, yes, I'd better."

Then she was off down the street.

Ruby went back and sat on the straw tick. She was smiling.

"What's funny?" Annie said.

"I think I just gave Frank Cord more grief than he's going to be able to handle."

Then she explained how much of a gossip her friend Mrs. Palmer was and that once she pulled her money from the bank, and once she told a few people about it—Cord would have a run on his bank and it would collapse before his eyes.

Now Annie smiled, too. "Ruby, that's the second best thing that could happen to that man."

"Except for being shot, of course."

Then they grabbed hands again and did something very much like a jig.

"Except for being shot, of course." Annie giggled.

Cord went to the hardware store and bought a big metal trunk, and then he went to the livery and picked out an especially sturdy farm wagon and told the man in charge to have it ready with a good team of horses at nightfall. Then he went over to the gunsmith's and bought himself two Remington repeaters with enough ammunition to start a small war, and then he went to the bank and appeared to be checking the lock on the back door.

Hanratty saw all this as he followed Cord around for the rest of the day. A few times Hanratty had to go to the toilet, and he was glad when Cord stopped in a place, because then Hanratty could find an outhouse and go fast and be back in time to pick up Cord again. A few times, too, he wondered if Cord might not be aware of him, because Cord would turn around quickly and for seemingly no reason and then Hanratty would have to duck his head or dive into a building front.

But then Cord would go on as if nothing were wrong, so Hanratty would start following him again.

There was an alley between the sheriff's office and a dry goods store next door and that's where Hanratty was at this very moment. . . .

Hanratty's left foot lifted off the ground in mid-stride.

His eyes fixed on the back of Cord's worsted suit jacket.

His mind hummed with all the juicy things he was going to have to report to the judge.

So there he was, his left foot lifted off the ground and—

A man who was built on the order of a safe appeared from the shallow shadows of the alley. He carried a very large Sharps rifle and without any hesitation at all, he walked right up to Hanratty and jammed the gun into his temple and said, "You're going to have to explain to Mr. Cord how come you're doing this."

Hanratty, shaken, could barely speak. "Doing what?"

"You shouldn't ought to do it. Follow a man and intrude on his privacy."

By now, of course, Cord had heard the commotion behind him and had turned around and was coming back.

Finally, Hanratty realized what had happened.

All the time he'd been following Cord, this most peculiar little man had been following him.

"Mr. Cord," the little man said in an almost childlike way, "I don't think you're going to like this one bit."

Baines said, "We need two tickets for Danton."

The swing station clerk wore a green eyeshade, fancy red arm garters, and a pair of false choppers that looked as if they could rend an antelope into large chunks.

159

"Danton, huh?"

"That seems to be the town I mentioned, yes."

For the first time the clerk glanced up from all his writing and stamping and said, "You fellas come down from the Point, didn't you?"

"Guess we did," Guild said mildly.

"Mind if I ask why you're on foot?"

"Mind if I ask why you want to know?"

There were four people in the log cabin swing station. Out back the Wells Fargo stage was in the process of changing horses, and two of the passengers were ladling some kind of stew out of a big pot. You could smell tomatoes and baked beans. The fresh driver was talking to the other two passengers about baseball.

"I guess that's a fair question," Guild said.

"Got to be careful. Lot of money on the stage. And a lot of robberies lately."

"Don't blame you for being careful," Guild said.

Baines, always a big help, had drifted over to the new driver and was listening hard to the baseball talk.

Guild said, "Baines, why don't you come over here a minute?"

Baines shot him an annoyed look. He wanted to talk about baseball.

Between teeth grinding uppers on lowers, Guild said, "Baines, get over here."

The clerk couldn't figure out what was going on.

Baines came over. It seemed as if some invisible hand were dragging him. "What?" he said.

"This man here would like to know why we're on foot."

"Oh," Baines said.

"He's afraid we're going to rob the stage."

Finally, Baines figured out what was going on.

They had planned to take over the stage somewhere

160

between here and Danton. It was going to have to be sooner than that. It was going to have to be now.

Baines said, "Now's as good a time as any."

So they both took out their guns, and Guild said, "How about you people quit talking about baseball and look over here a minute?"

Which they did.

"A goddamn highwayman," said a pompous man in a banker's black three-piece.

"Until about six hours ago, this man was a sheriff," Guild said.

"Actually, it was about five," Baines said.

"Until about five hours ago," Guild said, annoyed, "this man was a sheriff. And in a way I was a lawman, too. So we're not out to hurt anybody or even take any money."

"What exactly is going on here?" demanded the pompous man.

Guild said, "What's happening is that we're going to take the driver and the stage on into Danton. You'll all stay here. That way I can be sure you won't get hurt."

"You mean you're not robbing the stage?" asked the clerk.

"I told you, sir, no. We're commandeering the stage, using it as a way to get inside Danton and to the bank without being seen, but the driver and the money will be safe."

"Well for shit's sake," said the clerk. "Ain't that about the damndest thing you ever heard of?"

Baines said to the new driver, a paunchy man in a denim shirt and trousers and a battered, gray Stetson, "You're going to be all right."

"You promise? I got kids."

Guild looked at the driver who was being relieved. He was a scrawny man with a walleye.

"You have kids?" Guild asked him.

"Three of them," the man said.

"Bullroar," the clerk said. "He ain't even married."

"Then you're going to drive," Guild said. He looked to the door. "And now's as good a time as any."

"I really do got kids," the driver said. "Illegitimate ones that nobody knows about."

"Get out there," Guild said, gesturing with his Colt.

"What did the judge tell you?"

"Nothing."

"Come on, Hanratty. I don't want to hurt you."

"You couldn't hurt me," Hanratty said with some pride. "Least, not in a fair fight." Hanratty wore his thrice-broken nose proudly. "Or not without a gun."

"I don't want to hurt you, I just want to find out what the judge said."

"I told you. Nothing."

"You just start goddamn following me around because you don't have anything else to do?"

They had been in the basement of the bank for half an hour now. They were in a safety deposit room with heavy walls and a door an elephant could not knock down. They had Hanratty's hands tied to the back of the straight-back chair in which he sat. Through the barred, opaque window you could see the sunlight change subtly to dusk.

Cord said, "Hanratty, I'm going to ask you one more time. What did the judge say about me?"

Hanratty sighed. He looked comic, a man so big, a derby so small. It rested on his head like a derby on an organ grinder's monkey. "He just said to follow you. And report back."

"Report back what?"

"What I saw, is all."

Cord glanced at Kendricks, who stood with his arms folded across his chest. "So if I let you go, what would you tell the judge?"

Hanratty said, "I'd tell him just what I saw."

"What did you see?"

Hanratty's eyes swept the room. The wall of metal lock boxes. The wide table where you could sit to examine the contents of the boxes. It all had the air of a library.

Hanratty sighed. "What do you mean, what did I see?"

"Today. Following me. What did I do?"

"Well, you went to the livery and bought a wagon and to the hardware store and bought a trunk, and then you got some Remingtons."

"And?"

"And what?"

"And what does all that lead you to conclude, Hanratty?"

"Are you kidding me? You're planning some sort of getaway. I imagine you're going to fill up that trunk with money and get the hell out of here soon as it's nightfall."

"There," Cord said.

"There what?"

"That's what I wanted to hear you say."

"I don't follow you."

"Now that it's out in the open I can just turn you over to Kendricks here."

For the first time, you could see fear in Hanratty's eyes. Kendricks was a far, far different prospect from Frank Cord.

"Is that all right, Kendricks?"

"That's fine, Mr. Cord."

There was a knock, faint through the heavy door. Cord said, "Damn." He went to the door and pressed his head against it. To hear through it, he practically had to yell. "What is it?"

"You'd better come upstairs, Mr. Cord."

"What's wrong?"

You could hear the clerk on the other side laboring to be heard. "There is a group of people outside the door."

"The bank's closed. Has been for more than an hour. You know that, Bergen. What do they want?"

"They want you, sir."

"Shit," Cord said. He turned back to Kendricks. "I'm going to have to go up there and see what's going on." He put his head down, as if summoning all his strength, and said, "Did you finish that job for me?"

Kendricks nodded. "Yes, sir, I did."

"I appreciate it."

What Hanratty didn't know was that there were two trunks. One Cord had bought just today, but there was another one, too, and that one Kendricks had filled with all the greenbacks that had been in the vault upstairs. There was not the amount Cord would have wished for, but there was enough to escape with and live on comfortably for a time. Cord was beginning to see that waiting around for the Wells Fargo stage might be impossible. He might have to take the trunk upstairs and head directly for the livery now.

"I don't care what you do to him, just make sure he doesn't get away," Cord said.

"He won't get away."

Cord nodded and started to pull the thick door open.

Kendricks said, "There's something I should tell you. About the trunk I packed for you."

Cord turned around, curious. "Yes?"

"I kept Mr. Winters's portion back."

Cord almost laughed. What else could he expect from a loyal employee like Kendricks? "I understand."

"It's only right."

"Yes," Cord said, "I guess it is."

Then he went upstairs.

Chapter Twenty-Two

Guild rode shotgun on the stage till they got within a quarter mile of town, then he eased his gun over toward the driver and said, "Pull over here."

They stopped near a copse of birch trees. Guild said, "I want you to understand something.

"I'm going to get down and ride inside now. And if you try anything funny at all, I'll shoot you. Do you believe me?"

"Yes."

"Good. Because you should. Now let's get going to Danton."

He jumped down, got inside the stage. The seats were dusty and cracked.

Baines was rolling a cigarette. His weapon was on his lap. "The minute those damn deputies see us, they're going to open fire," he said.

"We're going to go right up to the bank. And right inside just like we're Wells Fargo guards. They won't know the difference till it's too late."

"I'm too old for this."

"You know why I'm so tired of hearing you say that?"

"Why?"

Guild said, "Because you and I are the same damn age."

Cord couldn't believe it.

In front of the bank had assembled a crowd that by now numbered in the dozens. In front, unconditional sourness obvious on her face, was Mrs. Palmer.

Which was just what he needed right now—a mob led by the orneriest woman in the Territory.

Cord let the curtain fall back in place. His chest tightened, and he automatically put out a hand to touch the region of his heart. For a moment, he closed his eyes and felt his entire body rock with the grief and fear of this moment.

All coming down.

He wished the wish of his boyhood—that somehow he could be transformed into his father.

His father would know what to do now. If it took violence, then there would be violence; if it took cunning, then there would be cunning.

But all Frank Cord could do was stand there, a kind of automatic sob traveling the length of his body, as if he were shedding somebody else's tears, shuddering now, hand spidery and out of control.

The money.

That's what he had to force himself to concentrate on.

The money.

"We know you're in there, Frank! You come out of there!"

No mistaking the voice. Mrs. Palmer's.

He pulled up the curtain again. Now Mrs. Palmer had led the men and women of the crowd right up onto the front steps of the bank.

"We want our money, Cord!" a man shouted.

Then the first rock crashed through the front window, glass flying in the dusk like colored pieces of crystal, scattering on the floor.

A second rock came soon after.

My father would know what to do.

"Are you all right, Mr. Cord?"

He snapped up straight, wondering how long Kendricks had been standing there. Kendricks looked at him, seeming to study him. His eyes lay especially long on Cord's twitching, spasticlike hand.

"Where the hell are the deputies?"

"Probably still patrolling the streets."

"We need them here. Fast."

"Yes, Mr. Cord, I'd say we do." He looked at where the rocks had smashed the windows. Outside now the crowd was chanting, *"We want our money."*

"Go get them," Cord said.

"Will you be all right alone?"

Cord listened for the taunt in Kendricks's voice. There was none. He was a dutiful soldier. He'd been paid and he was doing his job. He did not judge, not if you treated him right and paid him well enough.

Curious, Cord asked, "What did you do with Hanratty?"

Kendricks said, "I didn't kill him. Didn't have to. I just took a rifle butt and broke his kneecaps." He sounded pleased with himself, the way he might have sounded if he'd just saved Cord some money on a job. "I'll go now, if that's all right."

"Fine."

"Yes, sir. Things will work out, Mr. Cord. You'll see."

"Just hurry."

"Yes, sir."

He went out the back door. Cord followed him, closed

the door behind him, looked out. The rear of the bank was a big sandy lot. Kendricks drew his weapon, looked around, set off running.

Cord bolted the door then went over to the black trunk. He opened it up and stared inside at the rows of greenbacks. The payroll would double, if not triple this amount.

This time the rock came through the front door and it was followed by two men hurling themselves after it.

"Come out of there, Cord!" It was Mrs. Palmer again. "We want our money!"

Once more the two men threw themselves at the door. You could hear the hinges begin to give. They would not get through for a time, but they would get through sometime. If the deputies didn't get here soon.

Cord took a Remington and aimed it directly at the door.

If they got through, they were going to die for their trouble.

Annie said, "We've got to get out of here somehow."

From down the street they could hear the shouts of the crowd. The encouraging shouts.

Ruby went up to the bars, tried to shake them. "Damn," she said.

Annie could hear footsteps running by in the street outside. "At least I can watch," she said. She got up on one of the straw ticks and looked out. "Can you imagine, Ruby? They've got Cord trapped in his own bank." She couldn't have been more delighted at inheriting a treasure.

Then Annie said, "Oh, God, Ruby, come over here!"

She called out so plaintively, Ruby put her hands over her face and rushed to her. "What is it, Annie?"

"Out in the street! That nice Greek man back at the restaurant! Call him over here!"

"Let me up there," Ruby said.

Taking Annie's place, she pressed her face to the bars. "I don't see him."

"Keep looking."

"There he is!"

"Call him over. Maybe he'll help us."

So Ruby yelled for the Greek. At first he just kept up his fast pace down the boardwalk beneath the storefront awnings. But finally he turned and looked around, almost like a blind man, for the source of the sound.

"Ruby!" he said. "They got you locked up!"

"You feeling real brave today, Stamos."

He beat his chest magnificently. "Stamos is brave every day."

"Then you go around front and get the deputy to let us out. Could you do that, Stamos?"

"You watch," the Greek said.

Annie had scarcely finished asking, "You really think he can do it?" when they heard a crash coming from the front office of the jail. Moments later Stamos came trotting down the corridor between cells, the keys jangling free and lively in his brown fingers.

"How'd you do it?" Ruby asked merrily.

"It is all the surprise element, you know? I just come in and knock him out. Good thing he had a back to me."

Ruby laughed. "It's a wonderful thing he had his back to you, Stamos. It's a wonderful thing."

He let them out of their cell.

The wheel came off just as the team was pulling to reach Danton.

Guild was thrown against the opposite wall of the interior. Baines was thrown halfway out the door.

Guild was out in seconds, his gun in the face of the driver. "What the hell's going on?"

"You don't think I could throw a wheel on purpose, do you?" the man asked.

By now Guild was looking at Baines. "You all right?"

"Yes." He was kind of dusting himself off. Even now appearance mattered.

"Then get your ass over here and help us get that wheel back on," Guild said.

The deputy with the deep belly and the aged Sharps said, "You folks back away from there."

The crowd, which now numbered at least fifty, had fanned out in a wide circle in front of the bank. Street lights were on now, and the part of the crowd that was underneath the bank's gilt archway was in shadow.

"You heard me," the deputy said. He nodded to the other deputies. Each was rifle-armed and obviously ready.

One man in the crowd shouted, "There's more of us than them. Let's get them!"

But nobody moved. Not even the man who'd done the shouting. This was a crowd of merchants and workers and clerks.

Everybody knew these men by sight and not name, and knew they'd be happy to have an excuse to fire. There were at least ten of them.

Finally, Mrs. Palmer broke the silence, pushing her way back from the bank door to face the deputies fanned out in the streets.

She went up to one of them and said, "If you didn't have that rifle, I'd slap your face."

The man laughed.

The deep-bellied deputy stepped up to the crowd, cocked

170

his Sharps and said, "Now everybody here start moving. Get back to your homes."

For emphasis, he fired in the air.

The sound was enormous in the quiet of dusk.

The shot had its desired effect. It dispirited some, frightened others. Even if their money was at stake, it wasn't worth dying for.

Another deputy, monkey imitating monkey, let go with a shot, too. This one was more menacing, however. It chunked into a corner of the gilt trimming, just above the heads of several people, covering them with pieces of gilt and dust. A man started swearing sullenly, and a woman started crying.

"Now, move," the deputy said.

"It's a good thing my husband isn't alive," Mrs. Palmer said as she started walking down the boardwalk.

Cord let the curtain fall, closed his eyes, and took several deep breaths.

It was going to be all right.

He was going to get out of here.

An image of his daughters played reluctantly on the edge of his mind and for a time he gave himself up to memories of their smiles and tears and times together—then he shook his head and started to the back of the bank. It was too late now. Flight was the only thing left to him.

In the rear of the bank he heard the clatter of the farm wagon Kendricks was bringing around.

Cord went to the door, lifted the bar from its wedge, and said to one of the deputies outside, "How about giving me a hand?"

"Sure, Mr. Cord."

Before today, Frank Cord would not have spoken to a man as scruffy as this one.

171

The man came inside and together they hefted the black trunk and carried it outside and put it in the wagon bed. All the way out, Cord's nostrils were filled with the man's stench.

The wagon loaded, Kendricks came up. "Everything is ready." He nodded to the wagon. "If you don't mind my saying so, Mr. Cord, I think now would be a good time to leave."

"I know." He looked up at the sky, night now, stars out, fireflies on the silky darkness, crickets noisy in the shadows. He thought of a time when he was a boy—he'd played statue-statue with a girl till they'd both fallen down in each other's arms. He could still remember the thrill of that touch, and how good, unless his father was yelling at him, it had been to be young. . . .

"Are you all right, Mr. Cord?" Kendricks asked quietly.

Cord hadn't realized till now that tears were rolling down his cheeks. He wasn't even sure why.

And, Jesus, in front of a man like Kendricks.

"I have to go in and get my Remingtons," Cord said, "then I'll leave."

He spoke in a voice harsh as possible so Kendricks wouldn't think . . .

Jesus, crying in front of a man like Kendricks.

Cord went inside to get his rifles.

The small crowd was angry. Some swore. Some turned around and glared at the chunky deputy who forced them down the street, his rifle ready.

"Look!" Annie said.

"Quick," Ruby said, "in here."

There was a bakery storefront deep in shadows cast by the streetlights.

Annie and Ruby ran all the way back to the door and huddled in the gloom.

The crowd walked past. "Just keep movin' now," the deputy told them. He had a whiskey voice. When he reached the bakery, his Stetsoned head started to turn into the bakery entrance then pulled back to watch the crowd.

"Shoot," Ruby said, sighing.

"We got to hurry," Annie said, "I want to find Cord."

They started back onto the boardwalk again. Ruby checked out one direction, Annie the other. When they decided it was safe to go, Ruby said, "Annie?"

"What?"

Ruby took her hand. "You don't have to do this, you know, child."

"Yes, I do, Ruby, For Earle."

Ruby leaned forward and kissed her cheek. "Maybe you do after all, child. Maybe you do."

Annie took the Peacemaker from the waist of her butternuts. She'd found it in the sheriff's office. "You don't have to go, Ruby. Not if you don't want to."

Ruby's laugh crackled across the soft night. "Hell's bells, this is going to be the best story I ever covered. Now come on, girl. Come on."

They set off down the boardwalk. Around the corner they saw a derelict deputy in front of the bank. Sentry duty. He was sitting on the front steps, his rifle at his side. He was reading a paper.

"I hope that's the *Chronicle*," Ruby said.

"You think we can sneak down there?"

Ruby had her .44 she'd taken from the sheriff's office. "If he spots us, child, we've got to have the nerve to shoot him."

Annie said, "The only one I'm mad at is Cord. I don't know if I could shoot anybody else."

173

"All right then," Ruby said. "I'll fill him with lead and you can just watch to see how it's done."

"You really think you can do it?"

Ruby said, "I sure wish you hadn't asked me that question."

They started down the boardwalk, past storefronts, ducking into doorways when it seemed he might be looking up, walking on tippy-toe and holding their breath.

Then he did look up, and it was right when they were out in the open, a clear target for him.

The deputy dropped his paper, started to grab his rifle.

"I sure hope you can do it," Annie said.

"I sure hope I can, too," Ruby said.

She brought up the .44 the way she did at marksmanship contests at the fair, pulled back the hammer, and said, "May the good Lord forgive me."

"I'm sure He will, Ruby. I'm sure He will. But you better shoot now, don't you think? He's just about to point his rifle at us."

So Ruby let go.

The sound was sharp, echoing off the storefronts.

The deputy made the same sort of noise people did when they were drowning, a kind of gurgling, and then his rifle sort of flew up in the air slow motion and then fell to the earth and landed in the street.

By this time the deputy had already fallen to the boardwalk and clutched his chest.

"We best hurry," Ruby said.

They ran down the boardwalk the rest of the way to the bank.

When they reached the deputy, Annie looked down at the thick red blood pulsing from the man's chest and said, "Boy, Ruby, you sure got him."

Ruby said, "I don't think I want to look at him. He

might have kind eyes or something, and then I'd just feel like hell.''

Then they heard noises from around the back of the bank.

Annie said, "Cord."

"You be careful, Annie." Ruby shook her head. "I wish Guild were here to help us."

But Annie was already running around back. She had waited too many hours for this. All she could think of was Earle and what her life had been like before him and what her life was like after.

Cord had killed him.

Now she had to kill Cord.

She would never rest till she had.

She reached the clear, sandy area in back of the bank.

The first thing she saw was the farm wagon standing there in the moonlight. A team of heavy draught horses were hitched to the wagon, obviously ready to go.

On the seat of the wagon, the reins in his hands, was Frank Cord. Next to him stood a Remington repeater.

"How the hell did you get out of jail, Annie?"

But she did not want conversation. She walked toward Cord. She was starting to cry. All she said was, "You shouldn't have killed Earle."

She fired the first shot, but she wasn't good with firearms so it jumped in her hand. The bullet missed Cord by a foot.

He dove for the ground, taking his Remington with him as he did so.

Annie retreated slightly, crouching behind the edge of the building.

"You get the sonofabitch?" Ruby asked, coming up behind Annie and crouching, too.

"Ruby, I should have learned how to shoot instead of how to entertain men."

"You missed him?"

Annie, fighting tears of frustration, said, "I didn't even hit the damn wagon."

"We'll get him. Don't you worry."

They were quiet for a long minute. They were both out of breath and sweating. All they could hear was insects.

"You see him?" Ruby whispered, nodding to the wagon in front of them.

"No."

The horses neighed and raised big feet and swished tails and dropped dung. And the insects kept it up.

Then suddenly from behind them, somebody said, "You'd better put down those guns."

They whirled around and saw a short, massive man standing there.

Ruby didn't say anything. She just fired.

Even though the man had been holding a rifle, he apparently hadn't expected anything like this from these women.

His face vanished in blood and screams, and he fell to the ground, most profoundly aggrieved. She had shot him in the right eye, and the bullet had gone into the brain.

Then Annie turned back toward the wagon and that's when she saw Frank Cord standing there—obviously compelled to come out of hiding to see what had happened—and then she saw her chance.

Finally.

At last.

Her second and best opportunity to avenge Earle. She wouldn't miss this time.

She sighted along the barrel of the gun.

And Frank Cord raised his rifle and shot her three times right in the chest.

Nothing had ever prepared her for what came next—her body first hot then cold, sudden images of her real ma and then her ma of the good-luck locket and then of the man

176

who'd raised her and then of Earle and then one Christmas when Earle had stayed sober and they'd sung carols and the one Fourth of July when they'd watched fireworks so yellow and green and red and splendid against the velvet night sky. And all the time her body was hot and cold, cold and hot, and nothing had ever prepared her for this, the chills or the twitching or the way Ruby's voice was so faintly screaming and sobbing, sobbing and screaming, so distant. . . .

Chapter Twenty-Three

They came into Danton with the horses straining to keep up with the cracking demands of the driver, with the Wells Fargo coach trailing dust in the lamplit air, with Guild and Baines ready with their guns.

Half a block from the bank, past the first curious gazes of the roaming armed deputies, they saw Ruby Gillespie standing in the center of the street.

She looked dazed.

Her hands were held up in the air as if exhorting God to some unknown action.

"Here's the bank!" the driver shouted, beginning to brake the stage to a dusty halt.

"Did you see Ruby?" Guild said, as he got ready to push the door open when the coach came to a final stop. They would have to move fast, find Cord and capture or kill him.

"Yeah. I did. What's wrong with her?"

Guild, trembling, said, "I'm afraid I know."

The stage jerked to a stop.

"Ready?" Guild said. His voice was unsteady. He was thinking of Annie.

"Ready. And I'm not even afraid, Guild. Hell, I just hope I get a chance to shoot somebody. It's been a while." He smiled. "A man misses the simple things in life."

Guild opened his door. It creaked. He put one foot down, then the other. He surveyed the street for sign of deputies.

"Guild!"

The voice was sharp as a gun report across the canyon of the business district.

Ruby came toward him, her arms outstretched. Her sobbing told him the terrible news.

Ruby was twenty feet away when a man stepped out from next to the bank building and said, "Put down your arms, men."

Before Guild had time to twist and face the man, Baines squeezed off two shots.

The short, thick man with the odd face paused a moment, dropped his rifle to the ground, and then fell face forward.

Baines said, "I wish there was another one of the bastards around."

"She's dead, Guild," Ruby cried, falling into his arms.

He held her, the tender weight of her, the dignified age of her. "Jesus," he said, and she had to hold him in return. He felt his knees weaken a moment and a coldness pass through.

Then he said, "Where's Cord?"

"Out back. He's getting ready to leave." She nodded to the man Baines had just killed. "That was his bodyguard."

The team of big draught horses exploded from the alley paralleling the bank, and Guild and Ruby had to jump out of their way.

"Cord!" Ruby yelled.

The farm wagon flew out of the alley and into the street. In moments, it was lost in rolling clouds of dust.

"Stay with her, Baines," Guild said.

He ran down the boardwalk to the corner where the livery was. He ran inside, interrupting the blacksmith from his work.

The blacksmith said, "They're looking for you, mister."

Guild pulled the hammer back on his gun. "You got a wife?"

"Yeah."

"You want to see her again? Go over there and get that horse saddled. You got two minutes or I kill you."

"Bullshit. You wouldn't."

Guild kicked the man hard in the stomach. He doubled over. "You think I wouldn't?"

The man didn't say anything. He just went over and saddled the horse, a dun.

"Sorry I kicked you," Guild said.

"Yeah, I'll bet you are."

Guild rode out of the livery traveling faster than even the farm wagon had.

He was into a full gallop by the time he reached the main street. He rode past Baines and Ruby. Near the town limits a deputy saw him and dropped to one knee to get off a clear shot. Guild shot him in the throat.

The stage road twisted through birch and oak, tall grass and sandy areas. There was a half-moon overhead, and to his left, behind the trees and rolling hills, a river that smelled of fish. Cord was going fast enough that Guild couldn't even see his dust now.

Ten minutes later, the dun heavily sweated already, Guild saw the wagon. There was a depot five miles west. Now Guild knew where Cord was headed. The train.

Cord fired at him.

Guild didn't return fire, he just hung on to the saddlehorn and crouched down, using the body of the animal for a shield as much as possible.

180

Cord kept firing.

Once, the horse spooking, Guild feared he was going to be thrown off. He held tight, tried to calm the horse with pats and soft words in his ear.

Cord kept firing, first with a pistol and then with a rifle. They weren't good shots. He was firing because he knew it was over and there was nothing else he could do.

Then Guild's horse was shot in the flank and the animal reared and cried out, and Guild was thrown to the side of the road.

But he was angry instead of hurt. At least for now. He scrambled to his feet quickly and started running down the road after the retreating wagon.

Finally, he dropped to a knee, sighted carefully as possible, and put three bullets after the vanishing figure of Frank Cord.

There was a curve in the stage road, one lost in a hollow. The wagon vanished.

Guild stood in the dust, panting, his chest hurting from slamming into the ground a few minutes before. His mind was filled with images of Annie, especially of the time they'd been in bed together, her gentle voice and frail body there in the darkness.

Then he heard the crash.

It was about a quarter-mile ahead.

Laughing, he started trotting. He hurt too much to run, but he could trot. It took him ten minutes to find where the wagon had run off the road and crashed into a big oak.

The horses were struggling to get out of their traces.

Frank Cord, bloody, crazed, had crawled away from the wagon and opened up the trunk the wagon had borne.

He didn't hear Guild until the taller man was standing over him.

Guild eased the hammer back on his .44.

"Jesus Christ," Cord said, turning around, his eyes

white and haunted in the deep, moonlit shadows. "You wouldn't just gun me down, would you?"

Guild did not say anything.

He put two bullets in Frank Cord's face and two more in his heart.

Chapter Twenty-Four

They buried Annie next to Earle, and after Ruby threw roses on the newly dug grave, she looked up to Guild and said, "She cared about you, Guild."

He did not want to put too fine a point on it. "She cared about you, too, Ruby."

There was a breeze then off the creek below, and grass was on it and the soft smell of willows and the hard smell of white fir.

The collie that had been there the day they'd buried Earle appeared again on the hillock above them.

"He mustn't have a home," Ruby said.

Guild said, "Maybe he doesn't want one."

She stared at him. "Like you, Guild?"

He sighed. "Maybe so." Then he nodded to the creek where Baines waited with the horses. "He's a good man. He can help straighten this town out if you'll let him."

"Let him?" Ruby laughed. "Hell, I'll help him."

"Good," Guild said. He stared down at the wooden cross that was Annie's and for a moment closed his eyes and let the breeze balm him.

He felt Ruby touch his hand. He opened his eyes.

"I'll tell you what I used to tell my own kids."

"What's that?"

"Stick out your hand."

"What?"

"Stick out your hand and then open it up."

He did so.

"Now close your eyes again. I've got a surprise for you."

"You don't think I'm a little old for this?"

"Just goddamn do it, Guild, all right?"

So he did it.

"Now you can open your eyes."

Which he did.

There was Annie's heart-shaped locket.

"You keep it, Guild," Ruby said. "Take it with you."

"I'd like that," Guild said, putting it in his pocket.

He slid his arm around Ruby and they walked down the hill together.

About the Author

Edward Gorman is a Midwest advertising executive and writer who is known for his Jack Dwyer mystery novels ROUGH-CUT; NEW, IMPROVED MURDER; MURDER STRAIGHT UP; MURDER IN THE WINGS; and THE AUTUMN DEAD. He is also co-publisher of MYSTERY SCENE magazine and has recently edited THE BLACK LIZARD ANTHOLOGY OF CRIME FICTION.

Attention
Mystery
and Suspense
Fans

Do you want to complete your collection
of mystery and suspense stories
by some of your favorite authors?
John D. MacDonald, Helen MacInnes,
Dick Francis, Amanda Cross, Ruth
Rendell, Alistar MacLean, Erle Stanley
Gardner, Cornell Woolrich, among many
others, are included in Ballantine/
Fawcett's new Mystery Brochure.

For your FREE Mystery Brochure, fill in the
coupon below and mail it to: